BODY OF EVIDENCE
LENORA WORTH

Steeple
Hill®

Published by Steeple Hill Books™

Special thanks and acknowledgment to Lenora Worth
for her contribution to the Texas Ranger Justice miniseries.

STEEPLE HILL BOOKS

Steeple
Hill®

Recycling programs
for this product may
not exist in your area.

ISBN-13: 978-0-373-44429-8

BODY OF EVIDENCE

Copyright © 2011 by Harlequin Books S.A.

www.SteepleHill.com

Printed in U.S.A.

"You can't be too careful."

She turned toward the horses. "I'm so tired of hearing that."

Anderson whirled her around so quickly, she felt the rush of air passing over her face.

"Jennifer, this isn't a joke. It's real."

"You're scaring me, Anderson. And I've never been scared before."

Untying Sadie's rein and handing it to Jennifer, he said, "I get so caught up in the facts, I forget the reality of things like this. I get that you're used to being on your own and doing things your own way. But I took on this assignment for many reasons, one now being that I need to protect you whether you like it or not."

"Thank you. It's been a long time since anyone has bothered to worry about me."

Then she took off, leaving him sitting there on a stomping horse because she was too afraid to look back to see if he was following her.

TEXAS RANGER JUSTICE:
Keeping the Lone Star State safe

Books by Lenora Worth

LENORA WORTH

has written more than forty books for three different publishers. Her career with Steeple Hill Books spans close to fourteen years. Her very first Love Inspired title, *The Wedding Quilt,* won Affaire de Coeur's Best Inspirational for 1997, and *Logan's Child* won *RT Book Reviews*'s Best Love Inspired for 1998. With millions of books in print, Lenora continues to write for the Love Inspired and Love Inspired Suspense lines. Lenora also wrote a weekly opinion column for the local paper and worked freelance for years with a local magazine. She has now turned to full-time fiction writing and enjoying adventures with her retired husband, Don. Married for thirty-five years, they have two grown children. Lenora enjoys writing, reading and shopping...especially shoe shopping.

For by Him all things were created:
things in heaven and on earth, visible and invisible,
whether thrones or powers or rulers or authorities;
all things were created by Him and for Him.
—*Colossians* 1:15–16

To Tori Luce
Part tomboy and part girly girl!

ONE

She was caught between a hungry alligator named Boudreaux and a tall drink of water named Anderson. And they both had way too much attitude.

Jennifer Rodgers had had better days.

And worse ones, too, come to think of it. Someone didn't want her to build her alligators a fancy new pen. Maybe that was why the handsome Ranger, who'd discreetly flashed his badge for her eyes only, was here.

Deciding to do things in the order of greatest urgency, she ignored Mr. Tall, Blond and Texas while she finished feeding chunks of raw chicken to cranky old Boudreaux. It didn't take long for the younger alligator sharing this temporary pen with Boudreaux to slide toward the evening meal.

"C'mon, Bobby Wayne," Jennifer called. Tossing some of the meat toward shy Bobby Wayne, she smiled. "Don't worry, Boudreaux will save you a bite or two. I hope."

Boudreaux didn't seem worried about his buddy. He was too busy tearing at the meal. Jennifer threw the last of the bucket of stinky meat into the water hole then turned on the nearby spigot and pulled the big water hose toward the bucket to give it a good rinse. Then she pulled off the heavy rubber gloves she always wore to feed her animals and tossed them in the bucket. She'd soap the whole thing down later.

After she got rid of the Texas Ranger waiting a little too impatiently to talk to her.

Ranger Anderson Michaels used the time waiting at the Rodgers Exotic Animal Rescue Farm to analyze both the place and the woman running the big compound.

Jennifer Rodgers was cute and just about as exotic as some of her animals. Her long curly dark brown hair was caught up in a haphazard ponytail that kept shifting around to her face each time she leaned over. She was fit, her figure almost boyish, but Anderson could tell she was all woman even if she did have on grungy khaki pants and an old brown work shirt. Her brown eyes gave away her feminine charm. So did the way she grinned at that nasty-looking alligator lunging toward the meat she held down over the rickety old fence.

Surprised to see yet another gator opening his snout to snap at the raw chicken, Anderson strolled closer to the chain links surrounding the makeshift pond.

"Do they stay in there?" he asked, wondering if he could outrun old Boudreaux. He'd always heard an alligator could get up to forty miles per hour in speed. Anderson didn't want to test that theory.

Jennifer laughed, then turned to wipe her wet hands on a towel draped over a post. After pulling a small bottle of hand sanitizer out of the deep pocket of her baggy pants, she squirted some on her hands and rubbed them together. The fruity scent of the sanitizer filled the crisp October air while her laughter filled Anderson's head.

"Boudreaux is too old and lazy to even try and get out, but Bobby Wayne…well, let's just say he doesn't like surprises. Even though he's shy and reclusive at times, he's been known to turn aggressive if you look at him the wrong way."

Her expression challenged Anderson to do just that. And suggested she might do the same thing as the gator.

"I'll keep that in mind," Anderson said, grinning at her. "But right now, I need to talk to *you*."

Jennifer nodded, then started up the dirt lane toward the long square log cabin where, according to his notes, she worked and lived. "Is this about the incident with the fence on the back end of my property?"

Anderson's radar went up. "Has something happened back there already?"

She frowned. "Yes. I thought maybe that was why you were here. The local authorities said there wasn't much I could do but fix the fence."

Anderson's gut tightened. Had the cartel and the Lions already made her a target?

He glanced around, then pushed at his tan cowboy hat. A teenaged boy and a middle-age woman were working down a hill inside the goat pen and a few curious visitors milled around watching and asking questions about the "Closed for Renovations" sign. No one was paying him much attention. He'd purposely changed out of his official uniform into a sportscoat and jeans and his own hat. "Could we talk somewhere private?"

"Sure. I was just finishing up for the day, anyway." She nodded toward where the two other workers were busy with the goats. "That's Jacob—he's my part-timer and the woman with him is a volunteer. They'll close up and leave when they finish up with the goats." Giving him another bold stare, she said, "C'mon in and I'll pour you a cup of coffee."

Anderson looked toward the approaching orange-red sunset. "Sounds good. Now that the sun is setting, it's kind of nippy out here."

She pushed at the double screen doors on the long back porch, then guided him up a hall past the big open oak door that had a sign saying "Office". "Yep, after that rain earlier in the week, it's a little cool for October. Those two fellows out there will go into a kind of hibernation if it gets any colder. We've just started building them a new pond, so I hope to get them moved before winter sets in. That is, if I can stop whoever it is that keeps damaging what we've already built."

She motioned toward another open door. "This way. Coffee's in the kitchen. Oh, and I have a very old dog in here, but he probably won't move a muscle to bark at you." Pointing to the sand-colored dog on a plaid bed by the fireplace, she said, "Roscoe, this is Anderson. Say hi."

Roscoe opened his doleful brown eyes and grunted.

"Some watchdog."

"He used to be the best. But he's arthritic and ornery now. My dad gave him to me when I was a teenager. He keeps me company."

After offering Roscoe his knuckles to sniff, Anderson noted that the place wasn't all that secure. No alarm system that he could see. And standard windows and doors that creaked and groaned each time the wind hit them. Everything looked a little frayed and run-down, but the place was clean. Looking through the big open door toward the front, he noticed long shelves of supplies along with pamphlets about various animal causes lining the wall behind the battered desk. A standing sign gave the cost of daily tours, stating that all students got in free.

His advance research on her website mentioned an aviary, a turtle house and pond and several other outbuildings and animal shelters, including a barn and stables. And as she'd mentioned, he had discovered she was building a bigger, better pond for the alligators. Obviously, Jennifer Rodgers was as dedicated to protecting animals as her famous late father Martin had been.

But even though her site indicated donations were always needed and welcome, it looked like she was struggling to keep things going on this remote compound.

Anderson hated to add to her troubles, but she had to know she might be in danger, especially if someone had already messed with a fence. Her rescue farm was located in an isolated spot just off I-10, about twenty miles from San Antonio. A perfect location for a drop site in drug trafficking, just like the suspect they had in custody had claimed. And he wondered now if that new alligator compound was being built too close to the alleged drop site.

Jennifer poured two cups of coffee, then motioned to the rectangular dining table on one side of the big den behind the office room. "Take a load off. And start talking, Ranger."

Anderson watched as she turned her own chair around so she could straddle it, her hands dropping over the high back, her dark eyes centered on him.

Her fingernails were painted a brilliant candy-apple red.

Interesting. And distracting.

Taking off his hat, he ran a hand over his hair and pulled out a chair. "Ah, well, I'm here because we have reason to believe some suspicious activity has been transpiring on the south end of your property, Miss Rodgers."

She nodded. "Yes. The brand-new fence around the pond we're building back there was cut. It needs to be redone before we can get on with the construction. We just started last week, so I'm not happy about being set back already. I saw a man with a mustache running away, but I didn't get a good look at him."

"I'm not here about that, specifically," he said. "But this could be connected to my reasons for being here, Miss Rodgers. Did the man see you?"

"He glanced back at me, then ran." Her expression went still. "Call me Jennifer. And talk in plain English—not Ranger-speak, if you don't mind. What kind of suspicious activity?"

Anderson didn't need to tell her everything but he had to make her see this was important. And urgent. He only knew how to do that in Ranger-speak. But he tried to use layman's terms. "Our captain was murdered last month. You might have heard about it—Gregory Pike?"

"I read about it in the paper and saw the story on the news. His daughter found him, right?"

"Right. Corinna interrupted the murder and found another man unconscious beside her father. That man is still in a coma in the hospital but we've released his photo to the media, hoping to get a lead on his identity."

Pulling a copy of the picture out, he showed it to Jennifer. "Have you ever seen this man?"

She squinted toward the grainy picture of the unconscious dark-haired man with a scar on his face. "No. He looks rough. Hard to say. I don't think that's the man I saw the other day."

Anderson decided to go on that for now. Maybe she'd remember something once they got into the particulars.

Jennifer took a drink of her black coffee. "I'm sorry about your captain and that man in the picture. But I don't think it has anything to do with whoever cut my fence."

Anderson saw the impatience in her expression. He'd have to talk fast, he reckoned. "We managed to bring in a suspect, Eddie Jimenez, who was captured after breaking into Corinna Pike's house. He gave us information regarding a drop site—a designated meeting place where, allegedly, some Texas citizens are conspiring with a Mexican drug cartel. But he couldn't identify anybody. Or so he said."

Jennifer held out her hand. "Wait a minute. Are you saying what I think you're saying? Do you believe this drop site is on my property? That these drug runners are the ones trespassing back there? Are they the ones who messed up my fence?"

Anderson tried to answer all of her questions with one statement. "If someone's tampered with your fence, you can bet it's probably these criminals, yes, ma'am. And if that man thinks you saw him, he might come back."

She hit a palm on the table, causing Roscoe to open one eye. "And *that's* why you're here? Do you think *I* have something to do with all of this? I'm the one who called the local authorities but the deputy sheriff didn't seem all that concerned. Now you show up—obviously very concerned."

Anderson didn't think *she* was a suspect, but that couldn't be ruled out. "No, we don't think you're involved, but your property could be part of some illegal activity, and that activity could lead us to the man who murdered my captain. We need to keep tabs on your land, see who's coming and going. And that means I need to be on site for a few days. I'll call the sheriff and compare notes. I'll need a list of everyone who works with you and volunteers for you or any returning visitors who might seem suspicious."

Her eyebrows lifted like dark velvet butterfly wings. "As in—you want to hang around and...spy?"

Anderson wasn't one to mince words. "As in—I need to work here with you—undercover—until I can find out what's going on in the back forty."

She held so tight to her chair, Anderson thought she might snap the wood. "Say that again?"

"I need to go undercover, here on your compound, twenty-four-seven, for the next few days. I've been assigned to find out anything I can, based on the information the suspect taken into custody gave us. Which wasn't a whole lot, by the way. But if we couple that with your recent vandalism, I'd say something's going on here and we're on the right track."

She put one hand on the table then moved the other over her tousled ponytail. "So when you say go undercover, you mean you want to stay here and pretend to work for me while you're watching this property?"

Hadn't he just told her that? "That's it, yes, ma'am."

"Stop with the ma'am stuff, okay?"

"Okay, ma—" He smiled. "Okay, Jennifer. I noticed you have a bunkhouse for volunteers. I can stay there."

"We aren't using it right now, but yeah, you'd better believe you'll stay there. I don't like people underfoot."

Anderson could tell that. Her whole stance practically shouted for him to go away. "Are you here alone after hours?"

"I have the part-time helper you saw earlier—the kid who comes in after school. And a rotating list of volunteers. And we have a local vet who comes by about twice a week. Our work hours vary according to the animals' needs, of course." She shrugged. "But yes, for the most part, I'm here alone after hours. Just me and Roscoe there."

He noted the sadness and the resolve tracing through her eyes. "I'm sorry about what happened to your daddy in the Amazon. My mom used to watch his local show on one of the cable channels."

"Thank you." Jennifer looked down at the wooden table. "My father loved what he did and he taught me to feel the same way. I'm planning to honor his dream of making this place into a full-fledged exotic animal haven, with lots of hands-on teaching. You know, children touring the place, volunteers being able to educate people on endangered animals and how to protect them. We can learn a lot from nature and that was my dad's greatest hope.

"He wanted people to respect nature and abide by the laws set up to protect animals and he was well on his way to becoming known the world over for his work, but…now it's up to me. He left me a little money and I used part of it to buy up the acreage behind this place. Like I said earlier, I've already started clearing that area so we can build a better-equipped pen for the gators. I guess the drug runners beat me to it, but that—and a little vandalism—won't stop me from building my alligator preserve."

Anderson saw the passion and the sincerity in her eyes. She would work hard to complete her father's dream. And she might even do that at the risk of everything else, including her own safety.

"I think that's mighty admirable of you. And I don't want to interfere with that. But…you need to be careful. The people we're dealing with are ruthless and determined. They'll stop at nothing to keep moving drugs through Texas."

And he couldn't even tell her the worst of it—that the group pulling the strings was allegedly compiled of some prominent Texans calling themselves the Lions of Texas and they wanted to open the border between Mexico and Texas. Ridiculous, since it would require changing federal law and make their drug running all that much easier. "These people are powerful, Jennifer. Do you understand what I'm saying?"

"I think I do," she replied, getting up to take their cups to the sink. "Whether I like it or not, you're empowered by law to be on my property. I can't interfere with a Ranger case, and I can't allow vandalism on my property, but I have to tell you I don't like it one bit. And…*I* don't expect *you* to interfere with my work while you're here. I have to get that alligator pond built. The boys need more room and more fencing, for their protection and for the protection of people touring this place. I have all the proper licenses and permits, and I have non-profit status. I could lose that if I'm not up to code."

"I understand. I'm not here to shut you down or disturb your work. And I don't blame you for being a tad agitated, but I have to do my job."

"And I have to do mine, all bad guys aside. But you need to know something about me, Ranger Michaels. I don't back down easily." She whirled at the sink and gave him a level stare. "And…I know how to use just about every weapon known to man. My father taught me to take care of myself. So don't worry on my account."

Anderson nodded and refrained from suggesting that she shouldn't be so bold and brave in this case. But he knew that wouldn't do any good right now. He could tell she wasn't too keen on having him around. "Point taken. Now, if you could show me to the bunkhouse, I'll get settled in and report back to my captain that I'm here."

"Okay," she said, wiping her hands down her pants. "We'll get you situated, then you can come back for supper. I made some chili earlier and you're welcome to share it."

"Thanks." Anderson was hungry and he did need to talk to her about what she did around here, her routine, the people who came and went. Might as well do that over supper. "We can go over some things. I'll explain how I'll go about my work and what you need to do to help me."

She grabbed a set of keys off a peg by the door. "Sounds fair, since I have to protect and care for my animals. So I intend to go over my rules with you and I expect you to abide by those rules at all times. Think you can handle that, Ranger?"

Anderson put on his hat and tipped it toward her. "Yes, *ma'am*."

She didn't frown at the exaggerated answer as he'd expected. Instead, she grinned and pointed toward a side door. "Right this way, *sir*."

Anderson smiled as he watched her prancing in front of him, her old Frye boots clicking with each step.

He'd sure have his work cut out for him, trying to run down a cartel and trying to keep this woman safe at the same time. It might turn out to be a lot harder than he'd planned. And a whole lot more interesting.

TWO

The man sure came prepared.

Jennifer watched as he lugged in a laptop, digital cameras, a recorder, a set of high-powered binoculars and a set of various flashlights. Not to mention the 12-gauge Remington shotgun, the Ruger Mini-14 automatic rifle and the slick, black pistol peeking out from his shoulder holster. And all the while his star-shaped silver badge, forged in the Ranger tradition from the *cinco peso*—a Mexican coin—winked over his heart at her each time his jacket fell open.

Even though he was dressed like any Texas man might be, Ranger Anderson Michaels wore the badge well and fit the bill from the top of his tan hat to the bottom of his Tony Lama boots. Jennifer watched as he purposely and meticulously placed his equipment on the shelves near one of the three bunks in the long, lonely room.

Forget the equipment inventory or the fact that she seriously needed to renovate this place. She rather liked surveying the man. Tall and built—nice. Crisp curls of wispy dark blond hair cut close to his head—nice. Wrangler jeans with a knife-pressed crease over rich brown no-nonsense boots—impressive. White button-down shirt with a hint of Western stitching around the collar and cuffs—sigh. And a brushed-suede, burnished-tan sportscoat that looked adorably worn in all the right places, especially over the broad shoulders—double sigh.

And each time he shifted his arms to put away something, she also saw the gun holster underneath his jacket.

"I guess I'm settled in."

Jennifer lifted her head to find Anderson staring at her with those golden-brown cougar eyes and immediately felt like a nocturnal creature staring into a forbidden window.

Wishing she hadn't impulsively asked him to dinner, she said, "Oh, right. I guess you are. I'll just go and heat up that chili."

He gave her a little half smile. "I'll get freshened up, make some calls and be back at the main house in about half an hour."

"That should work."

That would give Jennifer time to wipe this silly schoolgirl fuzziness right out of her brain. The man was here to do a job and from the looks of things, he was so focused and single-minded, he probably hadn't even noticed she was a woman. Too bad she had her own work to concentrate on. Or maybe, a good thing she did have work to concentrate on. 'Cause she sure didn't need to walk around sighing about a good-looking Ranger. Hadn't she learned from her parents' divorce that good-looking, adrenaline-junkie-type men didn't make great husband material?

Yes, she certainly had, and she would bet the farm that Anderson Michaels got a rush out of fighting crime much in the same way her dynamic father had gotten a rush out of stalking snakes and alligators. That didn't leave much room for home and hearth.

She only wished she could tell her girlfriends about Anderson next time they headed in to San Antonio for a girl's night out.

Anderson looked out the window of the bleak bunkhouse, watching Jennifer walk back to the main cabin. Only one security light for the whole place and it was as weak as a flickering candle at that. Did the woman even think about her own safety at all? She was a sitting duck out here alone at night with drug runners in her backyard.

Anderson didn't want to think what might happen if Jennifer tried to tangle with these nasty squatters. He'd seen enough crime scenes involving drug wars to know the drill—torture, mutilations and slow, horrible deaths. He couldn't imagine that happening to this woman.

Even though he was here to watch and observe, he wouldn't *let* that happen to Jennifer Rodgers.

So he checked in with his new captain, Ben Fritz, trying to stay focused on the case. "Yeah, it's me. I'm at the rescue farm and in the bunkhouse. As a courtesy, I alerted the local sheriff, too. He wasn't too keen on not being in on the investigation, but I'm hopeful he'll stay out of the way unless needed. As for Jennifer Rodgers, it was a hard sell, but for now I'm on the case. And not a minute too soon. She said someone's been messing with a new alligator pen she's just started building on the back of her property. This place is sure off the beaten path and has about as much security as an open-air flea market. Easy pickings."

He heard Ben let out a breath. "Be careful. Just watch and learn for now. We need to find out if anyone around there has seen either Eddie Jimenez or our mysterious coma victim. Or anyone else we can tie to this case, for that matter. And remember, I want you to follow up on any leads we get from that photo we released of our comatose suspect."

"Got it." Anderson planned to lock and load, too, if need be. "I can tell you right now, the place is way too isolated for my tastes. A woman alone out here—"

"Careful, buddy. That woman might think she has it all under control. You can advise her, but it's up to her to listen."

"Yeah, well, these are dangerous thugs. They don't respect women."

"I know that and so do you. Part of your job is to convince said woman of that. And your main reason for being there is to try and catch these thugs in the act, not become a bodyguard."

"I always get the hard cases."

"You're good at the hard cases. Just keep the drop site under surveillance and see if there's been any recent activity, maybe talk to some of the neighbors and the workers. Look for any kind of evidence we might use. Then wait and see if we get any more activity out there."

"I plan to go out to the site as soon as possible," Anderson replied. "According to what she told me tonight, things are already heating up around here. She

saw a man running away from a cut fence the other day.
Could get dicey."

"Keep an eye on her. Those drug runners won't like
anyone messing around in what they consider their territory. And neither will the Lions if they get wind of
this. If they risk showing up again back there, we have
to catch 'em in the act."

"I thought I wasn't a bodyguard."

"Not yet. But you can't stand by and let her walk
right into the middle of this, either."

"Got it."

Anderson put away his cell, thinking Ben was a fine
one to talk about stubborn, independent women. He was
so in love with Corinna Pike it wasn't funny. But it was
sweet and nice, if you went for that kind of thing. Anderson was too married to his work for such nonsense, or
so his mother and his baby sister told him with disgust
each time the family had Sunday dinner.

"One day, son, that tune's gonna change into a whole
different melody," his mother would always say. "Then
we'll be hearing the 'Wedding March.'"

Jennifer Rodgers came to mind.

"Maybe one day, Mama."

But not today. And not anytime soon. Anderson had
a strict code that required he stay focused on the case.
He'd learned early on that being a Ranger was tough
on family life. So he just played at dating here and
there, mostly when his mother would force some nice
woman on him. Never worked out. They usually ran
away screaming because of his heavy work schedule
and his inability to commit.

So his rule was steadfast. Get in, get the job done and keep moving.

His goal while here was to find out as much as he could about the drug runners using this land and to hopefully catch one or two. Catching one of the Lions of Texas would be even better since the Rangers had a hunch that some of the Lions often met up with the lower cartel members back there. Couple that with trying to protect a stubborn woman and, well, Anderson would be busy around the clock. No time for a love life.

His stomach growled, reminding him of that chili up at the cabin. Looking around, Anderson decided he could do all right in the austere confines of this old bunkhouse. The dusty, outdated place wasn't user-friendly in a cozy kind of way, but it was functional, and besides, he planned to spend most of his nights out on the property.

A mean late-fall wind howled and hollered through the open pasture across from the cabin. It had already been a rainy week and from the look of those dark clouds over the horizon, more rain might come. Anderson followed the aged, worn trail past the many out-buildings and animal pens, noticing smoke curling from the big chimney. That did look cozy.

He'd studied this track of land, using old maps and internet sites to clarify just how much additional land Jennifer had bought up after Martin Rodgers' death in a boating accident on the Amazon River. From what Anderson could tell, she'd had a fairly large piece of property to begin with but she'd added around twenty-five additional acres. Anderson would have to find the seller and ask that person about any suspicious activities, too.

"Wonder where her mother is?" Anderson muttered to himself while he tapped mud off his boots, then knocked on the side door at the back of the cabin. Another question to ask, he thought.

Jennifer opened the door without even looking out.

"You need to check who's here before you unlock the door," Anderson said by way of a greeting.

"You need to remember I'm not used to having people here for supper. I knew it was you."

"How'd you know?"

"Because everyone else has left for the day and you're the only other person here."

Stubborn had just met up with Stubborn, Anderson decided. "Do I need to remind you *why* I'm here?"

She waved him to the table. "No. I pretty much got that earlier. No need to go over it again."

"But there is a need for you to be more aware and a lot more careful. You might think you can handle any intruders but this is the big league. If they even suspect you might be on to them, you'll be at the top of their hit list. You saw a man back there, so that's one concern."

"Duly noted, Ranger-man." Then she made a face. "I have enough run-ins with mangy varmints on four legs, let alone two-legged critters. That man could have been after an exotic animal. Happens a lot."

Anderson chuckled in spite of his concerns, but the confidence in her gaze scared him to the bone. How did she do that? Say something cute and funny and make him laugh in spite of the seriousness of this situation.

He didn't like to laugh on the job. He rarely had any reason to laugh on the job.

"You are human, aren't you?" she asked as she ladled up two steaming bowls of chili that smelled so good his stomach growled again. Only, he couldn't see any meat in this chili.

"Yes, I'm human and I'm hungry," he said, grabbing a chunk of cornbread while he hoped the meat was swimming in the bottom of his bowl. Then he stood up. "Sorry. I thought you were ready to dig in."

She giggled, then sat down. "I am. But don't wait on me, cowboy. Eat your dinner."

But Anderson did wait. His mama had taught him manners, after all. And the isolation here told him to be cautious. Not only about the drug runners, but also about how he handled this. He was alone with a pretty woman. Hadn't seen that coming when he'd been assigned this case.

But his mother had also taught him to be a gentleman. And he'd rather spit dirt than disappoint his mama.

But he could enjoy the company of a woman, right?

Yeah, as long as he remained professional at all times. He said a quick silent blessing of the food with a little plea for guidance thrown in for good measure.

A few minutes later, Jennifer looked up at him while she chewed on her chili. "Is that tea okay?"

Anderson took a sip. "Yep. Tastes good." Then he shrugged. "It's a tad weaker than I'm used to, though."

"It's green tea. Has a lot of antioxidants."

Anderson eyed the green-gold liquid. "You don't say." He wasn't quite sure what an antioxidant was, but he had a feeling it didn't involve red meat and chuck wagon chow.

And neither did this strange chili. "Uh, this is good but—"

"I'm a vegetarian," she said, grinning. "So no, my chili doesn't have big chunks of meat. Is that a problem?"

Anderson could see the dare in her dark eyes. "No, ma'am. Not at all. Just happy to get a meal."

She must have seen the confusion on his face. "You don't drink green tea, either, do you?"

He shook his head. "Mostly coffee and water, and a soda now and then. I do drink sweet dark tea. My mama makes the best—"

"This will make you healthier."

"I'm already healthy."

"I can see that."

He stopped eating to give her a good long look.

And watched her blush becomingly.

Back to business, Anderson, he told himself.

He tried to sound gruff. "So…let's go over the ground rules about this new alligator pond."

"No rules there. It has to be built. The one I have the boys in now is not up to code. And I can't let school children in here for educational tours until I have a proper pen for those alligators. The new one will have a strong double chain-link fence around it and plenty of open spots for sunning, plus a deeper watering hole so they can relax and hide out if they want. I purposely put it back from the rest of the animals so we'd all be a little safer. Especially my turtles."

"That all sounds great for 'the boys' but we might need to warn your workers to be alert back there."

"We can do that. They sometimes carry guns anyway—you know, snakes, coyotes and such. They mostly shoot in the air to scare any unwanted visitors away."

"I don't want a shoot-out of any kind, at least not between your workers and the drug cartel. Just tell them you need to know about any trespassers."

"Neither do I. I'll talk to them first thing in the morning. Or…whenever the construction crew shows back up. They move from job to job."

"So, nobody else has seen anything out of the ordinary that you know of, other than your fence being damaged?" He reached into the file folder he'd brought and showed her a picture of Eddie Jimenez.

"I don't recognize that man and if any of my workers have seen him, they haven't informed me about it. Of course, they work during daylight hours. I'd think drug runners would do their business after dark. But that wouldn't explain how my fence got cut. Of course, it was around dusk when I did one last check for the day."

"Yeah, so don't ever go back there alone after dark, okay?"

"I'm usually too tired to do anything other than come home and eat a bite, do paperwork, then go to bed."

"Got it. So tomorrow, you can show me around. I'd like to explore the entire acreage while I'm here. And I need to question the previous owner, too."

"Previous owner lives out of state. I'll give you his number. We can take the horses out. I need to check on a few things, anyway. I'll also give you the name and number of the Realtor who brokered the deal."

"We need to update your regular employees. Just tell them I'm here to help with security for the new pen."

"That won't be hard. No offense, but you shout law enforcement. So working security should appease them."

He held up a hand. "I'm in civilian clothes. Look, just remind them to keep an eye out. Tell them you suspect trespassers back there. If you can give me a list of names, I can do background checks on them, too."

"Yeah, right. My employees and volunteers are solid."

"I'm glad you can vouch for them but I have to explore every angle. You'd be surprised how many crimes are from an inside job."

She nodded. "We're very strict on the rules and regulations around here, so I'll tell them to cooperate. But back to that lot, Jacob and his friends used to hang out there. They like to ride their four-wheelers around my property, but I did warn him after the fence was cut. I'll do the same with the construction workers and the volunteers. I guess it pays to be on the lookout. Like I said, people have been known to try and steal animals, especially endangered or exotic animals, so that's a valid point. Will that work for you?"

"Fair enough. Now tell me, have you had any other strange things going on around here lately—things that you've noticed yourself but didn't talk to anyone about?"

She shook her head. "Not if you don't count Boudreaux and Bobby Wayne fighting now and again. Or the coyotes howling in the middle of the night. Or my turtles trying to escape their pen. Or the llama chasing my part-time helper. Or the goats escaping and eating all my potted plants. Nothing strange at all." Then she glanced up and away. "Or the neighbor who's protesting that new gator pen—nothing strange there. He just doesn't get animal rescue, I reckon." Her head came up. "Hey, maybe he sent that man to cut my fence."

"Tell me more about the neighbor," Anderson said. "And we'll talk about those ornery gators and turtles later."

"Ralph Chason? He moved next to me about two years ago. We got along fine—I mean we rarely see each other—until he found out I'd bought the extra land. He had a fit when he heard I was digging a pond back there."

"Why should that bother him?" Anderson asked, his radar going up.

She shrugged. "I think he likes to take long walks back there. He's kind of a loner, some sort of artist. He works with wood and I'm sure he gets a lot of it from back there. Maybe he thinks I won't allow him on the property. I do have to put up a double fence for safety purposes, but I'm willing to work with him about that."

"It's your land and your call," Anderson said, making notes in his pocket notepad. "I'll need to check on Mr. Chason, as your security consultant."

"Don't go getting him all in an uproar," she said, standing to remove their chili bowls. "Want some chocolate chip cookies and coffee?"

"Real cookies with real chocolate?"

She laughed out loud. "Yes, but they are made with wheat flour and organic brown sugar. You'll never know the difference."

Anderson looked her over. She was so innocent in her hospitality. As if she had a law officer eating at her table every night. Her ability to trust strangers scared him. "Yeah, I'd love a cookie and some coffee."

Anything to keep her talking. He needed her to remember as much as she could about the happenings around here. Because he had a feeling some things were going on right under her nose without her even paying much attention. Things much worse than a cut fence.

And that was not a good situation to be in. Not at all.

THREE

Jennifer always got up early since most of her animals needed a good breakfast. Apparently, Anderson Michaels rose early, too. She saw him out the window, walking the property fully dressed in the work clothes she'd given him last night, and sipping a cup of steaming coffee. She, on the other hand, had stumbled into the kitchen and looked out the window at the rising sun, her eyes bleary from lack of sleep, only to see him blocking the sun's warm rays.

Kind of nice to see a good-looking man standing there outside her window, the fall sunshine haloing around him like an aura. Nice to watch, but working with him would be a whole different thing. Thus, her lack of sleep. She'd worried and fretted most of the night about drug runners overtaking her property and a tall Texas Ranger hanging around for the next few days. Now the source of those dark thoughts stood out in her yard, ready to get down to business. And that meant she had to get in gear herself.

Gulping down her first cup of coffee, she hurried to get dressed. She had two volunteers coming to work the front counter and clean the supply closet and several more scheduled to help with the morning feedings and other maintenance work. Anderson wanted to brief all of them on the happenings and his presence here. They'd decided it made sense to alert everyone since Jennifer didn't want her volunteers or workers to unknowingly walk into something dangerous. And this way, Anderson could get a fix on any regulars who seemed suspicious or jittery around him.

After washing her face and brushing her teeth, she tossed on some sunscreen and some medicated lip tint, then came back into the kitchen to make a quick breakfast.

Should she invite him inside?

"Oh, why not. After all, the man 'works' for me now, right?" she told Roscoe.

Roscoe nibbled at his own breakfast, then lapped at his water before he headed back to his bed.

Jennifer went over to pet him. "You won't be here much longer, will you, boy?" She'd have to give him his arthritis medication a little later.

She didn't want to think about losing Roscoe. It had been hard enough to lose her father so suddenly. How could she survive her best friend, her dog, dying, too?

She wouldn't think about that. Dr. Jenkins was doing everything he could for Roscoe, but old age was catching up with her companion on a daily basis.

A knock at the back door caused her to spin around. Roscoe let out a feeble half bark then laid his head on his paws.

"Good morning," she said as she opened the door to Anderson. "Want some eggs and toast?"

"I don't want to be a bother but I don't have many

supplies in the bunkhouse yet, except some aged coffee I found in one of the cabinets, so I'd like breakfast." He took off his hat. "I forgot and wore this. Habit."

Jennifer took the hat, the warmth of it causing little sparkles of awareness to shoot up her arm. "I'll hang it on the hall tree over here by the fireplace. You can wear one of our baseball caps." She grabbed an old one off the hall tree. "It has our logo on it." And why did his cowboy hat look right at home amidst her array of scarves, coats and her own hats?

He immediately went to Roscoe and bent down to talk to the dog in soothing tones. "He must have been a contender when he was younger."

"He's a purebred golden retriever," she said, smiling at Roscoe. "So yes, he was awesome and spoiled rotten."

"Well, the old fellow needs to be spoiled. He's obviously had a good life with you here."

She motioned to the kitchen. "We weren't always here. We traveled a lot. After my parents divorced, my dad gave me Roscoe for my fourteenth birthday, I guess as a peace offering. That poor dog has been all over Texas and Louisiana. My mother never could find the right spot to settle. So we came back here a few years ago but…after Daddy died, she took off again. She's in Arkansas now."

"Sorry about the divorce," he said. "That's got to be hard on a child."

"It was. My mother never quite got over my father. Since he traveled so much, she stayed home for a long time. She's had a hard time since his death. We both have."

"Sounds like you've been through a lot."

She turned away from the sympathy in his eyes. How could she explain to this man that her father had been an adventurer first and a family man second? She imagined Anderson fell into that category, too, since his job was demanding and never-ending. "Well, I don't have time to dwell on that this morning."

"Can I help with breakfast?"

"Sit down," Jennifer replied. "I can manage a couple of eggs and toast. The toast might be burnt, however."

"Won't hurt me. I have an iron stomach."

She couldn't argue with that. At least, he looked lean and mean and made of steel. "How about you, Ranger-man? Tell me about your family."

Jennifer loved family stories. Her friends always teased her about that. But she loved listening to their parents talk about how they fell in love and why they'd managed to stay married through thick and thin. And always wondered why her parents hadn't done the same. Now she lived vicariously through her friends because she didn't expect her own happy ending.

Anderson settled in his chair and stared up at her. "I have two younger brothers in their twenties and a baby sister, who's sixteen. Talk about spoiled. We're close, I reckon. I mean, we have our spats like anybody but when push comes to shove—"

"You stick together," she said, tossing the words over her shoulder at him.

"Yes. Isn't that what families do?"

"I don't know," she replied, pouring eggs into the frying pan to scramble. "Mine didn't."

"My mama makes sure we do," he said, his tone

softening. "Church every Sunday and hard work on Monday. That's her favorite saying."

Jennifer turned to look at him. "You know, I believe in God, but church was never high on my parents' agenda. My dad believed the whole world was a cathedral and he loved to explore it. He believed God was right there in the waterfalls and the mountains, the rivers, the oceans. I guess that's how I learned about religion."

"And your mother?"

"The original free-spirited, new-wave hippie, fifty-five now but going on twenty-two."

"I see. And what about you *now?* Do you go to church?"

"Is that part of your job, Ranger? To show me the way?"

He looked sheepish, hung his head. "Sorry. I just thought—"

"Your eggs are ready," she said, without rancor. She should be rankled at his question but it didn't bother her. He was right. She should get back into church. "I've been so busy lately," she said with an inadequate shrug. "That's the only excuse I have."

"I had no place asking you that," he retorted, waiting for her to sit down. "Never mind me."

That would be hard to do, Jennifer decided as they ate their breakfast in silence. The man filled the room with a demanding presence, like a giant tiger staking a claim.

Finally, he said, "So what's your typical day like?"

"Now there's a subject I can handle," she replied. "Tell you what, rather than explain it, how about you give me time to instruct and update the two volunteers due in a few minutes. Then I'll take you on rounds with me and you can watch and learn. And I expect you to pull your weight, too, Ranger-man."

"Yes, ma'am," he said, getting up to help her clear the dishes. "Hard work on Monday."

"It's Wednesday," she quipped. "And still, it's hard work, every day, all day."

"I don't mind hard work. But I do have a problem with hardened criminals. By the way, I took a walk back to the new gator pond last night. Spent the night out there."

"You did? I guess you were serious about staking the place out. Anything happen?"

"Not a thing. Not yet. But we'll catch 'em." He winked at Roscoe.

Jennifer thought she saw the old dog wink back.

Two hours later, Anderson wondered how Jennifer managed to do it all. The woman was a bundle of energy, whirling from task to task with obsessive determination, her love for her animals as evident as her need to keep this place going. But even with a few volunteers, how long could she keep up this pace?

"So you do this every morning?" So far, they'd fed the alligators and the horses, washed down several small animal pens, spoon-fed a passel of hungry turtles—both land tortoises and more water-inclined sea and snapping turtles—mushy bits of dog food and handfuls of worms, cleaned out some of the box turtles' aquariums and checked on a wounded hawk in the aviary.

She let out a chuckle. "Tired, cowboy? Listen, this is just the beginning of my day. But, yes, I have to feed the animals every day either in the morning or at dusk, and with some of them, both. The horses like to be fed about three times per day. I get relieved about twice a month, thanks to the other animal lovers who support this place. Everyone has a job and we all stick to our jobs. I keep a tight schedule with the volunteers and the paid workers."

"You have a lot of animals," he replied, ticking them off on his hand. "Two pigs, three cows, four horses, two alligators, a whole slew of turtles, goats, a llama, ducks, geese, a hawk, several rabbits, two doves and Roscoe. It's like the twelve days of Christmas around here. Do you have a partridge in a pear tree, too?"

She laughed again then tossed back that shimmering mane of dark hair. "I just might. It's crazy, that's for sure. I never have enough time or money. And people bring me all kinds of animals—dogs, cats, raccoons, you name it. I can't keep some of them so I have to call the state wildlife department to come and get them. Breaks my heart, but I just don't have the funding and I have to adhere to state regulations."

He followed her toward the stables as she headed back by the various cages and pens toward the main house. "How do you make money?"

"I don't. I have a board of directors that oversees operations and decides my annual salary—which isn't much, let me tell you. I charge for tours but until I get everything up to state code with the gator pen, I can't conduct any tours for a while. I speak at schools and civic organizations, and that brings in some funding, and I have a few corporate sponsors. But my income is at a minimum at best."

"How do you get by, then?"

She stopped and pushed at her hair. "I have a trust fund. It's small, though. My parents set it up for me a long time ago and it grew over the years. After I got out of college, they turned it over to me."

"And now you use that to live? No wonder you gave up meat."

She gave him a stare that told him he was being too personal. "I get by, Anderson. And giving up meat was my choice when I was young. Don't worry."

He did worry, though. Getting by was one thing. Living like a miser was another. "You're gonna need a lot of funding to do everything you told me about. From what I could tell, digging that alligator pond is a big deal."

"Yes, that's true. And I'm working on funding for that. But if word gets out that a drug cartel uses my land for little get-togethers, I guess I can kiss that and my few sponsors goodbye, right along with the plans I've drawn up to overhaul this place."

"Let me worry about that, then," he replied, resolve coloring his tone. Since he'd already observed the two women who were in the office today as well as several of the other volunteers, he asked, "When does your part-time person come in?"

"After school, around three-thirty."

He noted that. "And the construction workers?"

"They show up when they're good and ready. They've got several jobs so like I told you last night, I have to wait my turn. Of course, now they'll have to repair the fence, too."

Anderson wondered if she let people walk all over

her, but remembered she could get in your face when she wanted to. Was she stalling on the work because of lack of funds?

Not your concern right now, he reminded himself. "So when can we take a ride out and look around? I might get a better angle in the daylight."

She tossed that hair again. "Well, I have to clean out the stables—the empty stalls are used for everything from isolating animals to storing supplies—and we'll need to eat a bite. We could take the horses and check the work on the new pen after Jacob gets here. We'll be able to ride the entire back part of the property, too."

"Sounds like a plan," Anderson said, glancing around. "I could either help with the stable or I can try and secure this place a little more. Add a few brighter lights here and there, make sure all the door locks are up to snuff."

"I can't pay for that."

"Don't worry about the pay right now."

"I don't take charity."

"But you take donations, right?"

She frowned. "Is that some kind of Ranger trick question?"

Anderson let out a grunt of irritation. "It's a simple question. You have sponsors and people who support this place, right?"

"Right."

"Well, then, add my name to the list. Besides, I have to look the part of a security expert."

She stopped next to a storage building and turned to the spigot and big industrial sink, then started dumping buckets off the wheeled wagon she'd used to feed the penned animals. "So you're an animal lover?"

"I am. I'm as fond of animals as the next man, I reckon. Although my tendency runs toward mutts instead of alligators. We have several interesting adopted dogs on our property."

"Well, in that case, thank you, Mr. Ranger-man, for your kind donations and…I'm sure Boudreaux and Bobby Wayne will appreciate it, too."

"And how about you? Will you appreciate it?"

"Of course I will," she said, her actions telling him she was chafing underneath his intense questions. Water splashed and gurgled as she moved the spray hose over her feeding buckets with a tad too much zest.

Anderson didn't know why he was pushing the issue. It was just a few light bulbs and some door locks. What did it matter whether she liked it or not? It was for her protection, not to win points with her. Besides, his main focus was that pond. If the cartel had already messed with her new fence, what would they do next? He had to be there to find out.

Wanting to prolong being around her in spite of her sensitivity to accepting help and in spite of his need to stay professional, he said, "I'll help you finish up with the horses and the stables so I can get used to things, then I'll make a list of what I need to fix this place up." He shrugged. "I do know my way around a stable and from first glance, this one looks to be really well-organized."

She finished spraying the buckets then motioned toward the big building. "But it could use some sprucing up. A group of horse lovers took it on when I started

renovating a couple of years ago. They made the groom-
ing buckets for each horse, organized the shelves and
cabinets in the tack room and they donated galvanized
trash cans for feed—to keep the other critters out. And
I have a leaf blower to get rid of dust and cobwebs."
Shaking her hands to dry them, she said, "Of course,
I stay so busy I don't have time to tidy things up every
day so it tends to get messy. I missed checking the tack
room yesterday, but my volunteers gave me an update
on the horses. I keep the tack room locked since I have
medicine for the animals in there."

"I'm impressed. I'll check everything out and see if
anything needs tweaking. That is, if you don't mind."

"I don't mind and I'm sorry if I got testy before,"
she retorted, pulling out a set of keys. "I'm learning to
accept help whether I like it or not." Motioning to him,
she walked around the side of the old barn. "If you'll
put up the equipment, I'll unlock the tack room door."

Anderson watched her take off, then he gathered
the clean buckets and put them back on the wagon and
followed her.

Jennifer's high-pitched shout caused him to let go
of the wagon and hurry into the big barn. He found her
at the door of the tack room, her hands covering her
mouth.

The room had been ransacked. Cabinet doors were
swung open to reveal ointments, medications and various insect repellants, all knocked over or rearranged.
The floor was covered with blankets and saddle pads,
bridles and halters. And all the books and papers that
had probably been on the desk were tossed aside.

"Somebody's already tried to spruce things up in

here," he said, taking in the scattered equipment and strewn papers. "Or does it always look like this?"

"It wasn't like this yesterday before closing or my volunteers would have reported it," she said, turning to him with her hands on her hips. "Did you do this, Anderson? Is that why you kept asking me about where I get my funding? You still think I might be involved with these criminals? Were you in here looking for evidence or something?"

Anderson would never understand the female logic or how a woman could ask so many questions at one time and expect a man to remember each one. Putting his hands on his hips, he said, "First, I asked about your funding because I was impressed with how you handle all of this and I wanted to help. And as far as trashing your place—now why would I do that and leave it like this? That would be pretty dumb on my part, wouldn't it?"

Jennifer frowned at him, then nodded. "Yeah, I guess it would." Letting out a huff of breath, she shook her head, then leaned back against the door. "I'm sorry. I'm just not used to being under scrutiny all the time. I keep jumping to the wrong conclusions about all of this and…about you."

Anderson heard the sincerity in her words and reminded himself he was a Christian after all. He couldn't lash out at her even if she did tend to read him the wrong way. "Understood."

She gave him an apologetic glance. "So I wonder who decided to reshuffle my already disorganized stuff."

Anderson studied the mess for a minute then said, "Someone who's looking for more than evidence against your operation, Jennifer. I think we've been hit again by one of the drug runners. Cutting the fence and now this. They've seen your work crew back there near their drop site and they're not happy about it."

"But why mess up the tack room?"

"They were probably trying to scare you, or maybe they think you have something of theirs. Something they left behind." He glanced around again. "Or, this could just be a deterrent, a way of keeping you occupied. Which means I need to get back out to the site as soon as possible."

She looked frightened for the first time since he'd arrived here. "And that makes me a target, right?"

He nodded. "You became a target the minute you bought that land and started building that pen. But this just upped the ante."

FOUR

Jennifer finished clearing the last of the horse stalls, her work a comfort that helped push away the uneasiness floating over her like dust balls. Looking around, she noted that the stable was clean now. That would last a couple of days then she'd have to do this all over again. Busy work tended to keep her mind off everything else and that was probably why she was right in the middle of a criminal investigation. She had a tendency to focus on one thing to the point of blocking out everything around her. She'd learned this technique after her parents had divorced. It was a coping mechanism, but now, it was bringing trouble to her door. She should have been more vigilant in guarding her property.

I don't have a life, she thought, gritting her teeth to that truth. She'd pretty much blocked out everything and everyone but her work. Even God.

"Might need to rethink that one," she mumbled to her gelding Chestnut. "I've sure had a wake-up call now and I hear you, Lord."

The big horse nosed at her arm, his deep brown eyes gazing down at her in expectation of either a treat or a rubdown.

Anderson peeped around a stall. "I've cleaned up the tack room, taken photos of the broken lock and a video overview for evidence, dusted it for prints and checked in with my captain to give a report. I've also written a report and I'll get that to him later. I doubt we'll find anything concrete as far as evidence since nothing seemed to jump out at me. I don't think they were looking for drugs. Your supplies seem to be intact, far as I can tell. The volunteers who worked in here yesterday indicated everything was fine when they left. I talked to them by phone a few minutes ago. Might want to go over what I inventoried, though."

Jennifer couldn't help the shiver moving up and down her spine. "I can't believe they'd be so bold as to come in here and try to destroy my tack room—the only room I lock. I've never considered locking things up at night—other than the cages so the animals can't get out, and the office and living quarters. We have a main gate and we shut this place up tight after hours, so I never worried about keeping humans out."

"These people aren't just bold. They're evil, Jennifer. They don't care about humanity except in regards to how much money they can make running drugs. And for you, that means they'll do whatever it takes to scare you—or worse. So you're gonna need to take some extra security measures for your own safety."

She put the rake back on its hook and rubbed the calluses on her hands. "I worry about my animals, Anderson. And I don't have enough funds to put in an elaborate security system."

"Worry about yourself first," he retorted, irritation lining his expression. "And let me worry about security for now. This is just the beginning. We need to get out to that site and look around. But first, I want to talk to your neighbor, Ralph Chason."

"You don't think he's behind this, do you?"

"I can't say for sure. But questioning him is the first priority since you mentioned he'd complained to you about the new pen. I can do that now and we'll take a ride out later, if that's okay with you."

She checked her watch. "Jacob should be here in a few minutes. Let's take a break and go up to the house and clean up. Then, after you get back from seeing Mr. Chason, we can head out. I'd feel better if Jacob is here with my volunteers."

"Okay." He helped her finish putting away cleaning supplies, then checked the stables once again. "I'll be more aware tonight since I didn't hear or see anything last night. Probably because they decided to target your barn, just as a scare tactic."

"That's dangerous—you sleeping out there."

Anderson's chuckle surprised her. "You know, *you* don't have to *worry* about me. This ain't my first rodeo."

She looked down at her dirty work boots. "I get that, Ranger-man. But like I told you earlier, I'm not used to this kind of thing. I won't have something happening to you while you're trying to help me."

"Comes with the job, I'm afraid. And it doesn't allow for much of a social life, either."

Taking that as a warning, she asked, "How long have you been a Ranger, anyway?"

He squinted toward the afternoon sun. "Three years. Got a degree in criminal justice from Sam Houston

University, started out in the local sheriff's department, then signed on as a state trooper. Worked there almost nine years before joining Company D."

She did the math on that. He was probably a few years older than her twenty-eight years. And obviously not married and settled. "Did you always want to work in law enforcement?"

"Pretty much. I watched a lot of westerns growing up and I wanted to be one of the good guys. Being a Ranger seemed to fit the criteria."

Jennifer could see that clearly enough. He wasn't exactly Dudley Do-Right, but he wasn't Judge Roy Bean, either. She could tell Anderson's sense of justice ran deep and probably settled somewhere between being squeaky clean and getting down and dirty. In other words, a man she could trust to do the right thing.

Now if she could just trust herself around the man.

"How long do you think I'll be under lock and key?"

He looked around the property. "If I have my way, the rest of your natural born days. This place is isolated and it's an easy target for anyone wanting to break the law. Until you get your animal farm renovated and primed with better security and crowded with people again, you're exposed to all sorts of activities."

"Stop scaring me," she said when they reached the back porch. "You said yourself mean old Mr. Chason could have messed with the fence."

"I did, but why would a disgruntled neighbor go through your tack room?"

"Maybe he was looking for something to give to

the state so I'd lose my license and permits. I don't know."

"He's a suspect, too, far as I'm concerned. But we can't rule out the cartel, either. He might even be involved with them."

Jennifer didn't like that. She didn't like any of this. "I've lived here by myself since the last time my mother decided it was time to move on. I went to college and I studied hard—marine biology and animal husbandry. And I took management and business courses because I always knew I wanted to work in animal rescue. I'd already learned what I needed to know about animals from my father and from working side by side with my parents right here, before things got so bad between them. He left after the divorce and she stayed. So when I came back after the funeral and found my mother packing, I told her I wasn't leaving. And I don't intend to leave. But I don't want this constant threat hanging over me, either. So I'm more than willing to get with the program." She let out a long breath. "Besides, the drug cartel probably didn't even consider bothering me until I bought up that land."

"You're right there. You got too close to their little hideout and that's what concerns me. Building back there stirred up a hornet's nest. I can't decide if they're just messing with you or if there's more to it."

"Well, you found out whatever they're doing, thankfully."

"We got lucky with one of their minions. If he hadn't talked, I wouldn't be here, and you could be in serious trouble."

Her hand on the door, she turned to him. "I am grateful that you showed up. I would have been clueless. I tend to have a one-track mind when it comes to my work."

He tilted his chin in acknowledgment, then took off the khaki ball cap she'd lent him. "Well, that makes two of us. I won't stop until I catch up with these people. They murdered a good man. I had to stand there at his funeral and witness his daughter's grief and deal with my own heartache. We're all still reeling from this. So you can rest assured we both have the same goal here—to stop them once and for all."

"And this is just day one," Jennifer said, shaking her head. "Do you think they know you're here?"

"I can't say. I was careful last night, so they shouldn't, but then, these people always seem to be one step ahead of us."

"What could they want from me? Why not just do their drop thing somewhere else and leave me alone?"

He leaned close, his eyes deepening to an earthy gold-brown. "They want to make sure you don't see or hear anything back there that could put their operation in jeopardy, or lead the authorities to them. But they apparently have a good reason for coming back."

Jennifer leaned against the porch railing, her pulse galloping with fear. "They could kill me."

He came to stand by her. "Yes, they could kill you."

Anderson watched later as Jacob went around to each large pen to help Jennifer with the afternoon feedings. The kid seemed kind of skittish but Anderson attributed that to being a teenager. Teenagers didn't like being around authority figures. The kid could be hiding something. Anderson let the boy stew. Until he had a handle on this thing, everyone was suspect. Teenagers were easily swayed these days. Too many temptations.

And since he hadn't found anyone at home at the Chason ranch down the road, Anderson was in the mood to interrogate anyone who happened to be walking by. Jacob fit the bill.

He ambled up to the red-tailed hawk's cage to try some conversation. "So Jennifer tells me you plan on going to college in Austin. Have you decided on a major?"

Jacob went inside the big cage and closed the door, then held up a treat for the hawk named Abe. Abe lifted gracefully across the small space and landed on the gloved hand Jacob held at his side. "I dunno. Maybe economics."

"Economics—not my thing but a necessity in life."

Jacob grinned at that. "I like this job, but Jennifer says the pay will never be great. She said I could work at a big zoo maybe, but I'd have to take courses in that area, too. I'm not so hot in science and biology."

Warming up to the boy, Anderson went on. "She said you and your friends take the four-wheelers to the back side of the property sometimes."

Jacob gave Abe another treat then let the big bird fly back to his perch. Jennifer was waiting until the hawk's foot healed before they released him back into the wild where he'd eat mice and follow farmers, looking for grubs.

The boy turned to stare at Anderson, his expression

bordering on scared. "Jennifer gave us the okay until the other day when she found the fence all messed up."

Anderson nodded. "She doesn't want you to run into anyone dangerous back there. Y'all should find another place to ride. Have you seen anything unusual back there?"

Jacob shot him a questioning look then went into skittish mode again. "Like what?"

"Other people," Anderson said. "I'm here to make this place more secure. And one of the concerns I have is the openness of this place. Easy for vagrants to hang around."

Jacob looked away, then he shifted his feet. "That mean neighbor of hers—old man Chason—got on to us once when we were doing wheelies back there. Said we needed to stay off that property and he didn't care if Jennifer had given us permission."

"I see." Anderson almost took out his notepad, but refrained. He got the feeling Jacob wasn't telling him everything, but then, he wasn't telling the boy everything he knew or that he'd tried to question Chason earlier. "Jennifer and I need to take a ride back there. Think you can handle things here?"

"Sure," the boy replied. "She leaves things with me sometimes when she goes for supplies or goes out to dinner with her friends."

Interesting, Anderson thought, losing focus on his interrogation. "I'd never guess she leaves this place at all."

Jacob bobbed his head. "She gets all gussied up and heads into Austin or San Antonio sometimes. Likes to make the rounds on the Riverwalk. You know, eat some good Mexican food and shop or maybe catch a movie, usually one of those sappy romantic comedy things."

"Never would have figured she likes to shop, either."

Jacob snorted at that. "Are you kidding? She's a girl. They all like to shop. But hey, she doesn't buy a lot of personal stuff. She gets a lot of her clothes at second-hand shops."

"How do you know all of this?"

"She talks to me, just small talk," Jacob admitted. "And her friends come out and help sometimes on the weekends and I hear them comparing notes. But Jennifer spends most of her money on this place. And lately, she hasn't been going anywhere much."

Anderson was learning a lot about Jennifer Rodgers. And each tidbit was surprising. That explained the pretty fingernail polish. And gave him hope that he might be able to take her out to dinner when this was over. She deserved that much from him, at least.

Anderson grinned at the boy. "You just never know about people, huh?"

Jacob shrugged. "I'm learning a lot, hanging around her and her friends. They give me advice on girls all the time. But I still haven't figured women out."

"Nor will you ever, friend," Anderson said with a chuckle. He needed to remember that himself.

"I hear that," Jacob replied, flashing a reluctant grin.

"What are you two laughing at?" Jennifer asked as she came around the corner, dragging her little bucket wagon with her.

Anderson noticed again how cute she was in her

faded jeans and khaki work shirt underneath a brown hoodie. And those aged boots made her look more feminine than tough.

Jacob gave her a toothy smile. "I was telling him about how you like to get all fancy and head into town."

She looked embarrassed, then she looked stern. "Jacob, I don't pay you to gossip about my private life."

The boy looked shocked until he saw the smile twitching at her lips. "Sorry," he said with a sheepish grin. "I'll get back to work."

She winked at Anderson. "Good. And just to punish you, I'll let you feed Boudreaux and Bobby Wayne while we take the horses out for a ride."

Jacob perked up at that. "I get to feed the gators?"

"Only if you promise to stay behind the fence and be very careful. I mean it. Don't go inside. Just throw the meat over the gate, okay?"

"But what about the drop pole?"

"No drop pole unless we're both here. And one of the volunteers will be monitoring you, just in case."

"Okay." He finished up with Abe, leaving the big avian to stare after him as he left the cage.

"Seems like a good kid," Anderson said after helping her put away the rest of the feed buckets. "How long's he worked for you?"

"Almost since the beginning," Jennifer said. "I needed someone and a friend told me about Jacob. He wanted after school work and he'd just turned fourteen. So I hired him one summer and it worked out great. He'll be gone in another year, though."

They walked back down the path behind the house toward the stable. "So you like to go out on the town sometimes."

She gave him a wide-eyed stare. "And?"

"And…nothing. I'm glad to know you take a break now and then."

"Well, I haven't in a while. All my friends keep calling to check on me. But I want to get that pen finished and then I can relax." Then she stopped and put her hands on her hips. "Oh, wait, I can relax after the pen is built and after the drug runners are taken away and you're no longer in my hair. Then I'll be able to have fun again."

Anderson went into the stables with her, the smell of fresh hay and horses making him homesick for his own family ranch. Thinking he sure didn't mind being around her all the time, he said, "Maybe that will be sooner than later." Then he turned to face her. "And after this is over—"

"We'll both have to get back to work," she finished.

Leaving no room for dinner out or anything else as far as Anderson could see.

FIVE

"You have some prime horses," Anderson said, trotting Chestnut down the long lane toward the unfinished alligator pond. "This is one hard-working quarter horse. Did your daddy teach you about horses, too?"

Jennifer patted the mare she called Sadie, then shook her head. "No, my mother is the horse expert. Suzanne Myers Rodgers. You might have heard of her, or rather, your parents might remember her. She used to compete in shows on both the state and national levels. She was poised for a shot at the Olympics when she met my daddy."

"And?"

"And she fell in love and gave it all up, much to the disgust of her old-money-Texas-born-and-raised parents."

Anderson sat up on his horse. "Myers. As in Houston oil Myers?"

"The very ones," Jennifer replied, galloping along beside him. "My maternal grandparents, although I've never met them. They disowned my mother when she left behind college, dressage and the cotillion to marry my father."

Anderson whistled low. "You're kidding me, right? You don't even know your own grandparents?"

"Not on my mother's side. And my father's parents died when I was in grade school, first my grandmother, then my grandfather a year or so later."

No wonder she didn't trust anyone. No wonder she'd fallen away from her faith. The woman was pretty much on her own here. She'd tried to tell him that. She'd probably tried to explain that to God, too.

Now we're both here and listening, he thought. He prayed that God would hear Jennifer's cynical appeals.

"So you don't know your grandparents and you never hear much from your mother. That's not right, Jennifer."

She slanted him a harsh look. "Seriously, Ranger-man, I agree it's not right. But it's just a way of life for me. I'm used to it, so don't feel sorry for me, okay?"

"I feel sorry that your uppity grandparents don't have the sense of a goose or the grace that God grants all of us. I feel sorry that your mother is so self-centered and—whatever she is—that she isn't here supporting her daughter. I just don't get any of this."

Jennifer's expression changed from relaxed to perplexed in seconds. Her anger came through loud and clear in her next words. "That's because you have a tight-knit family, Anderson. You've never been through the stuff I've had to endure. But hey, I'm okay. I'm doing just fine on my own. I don't need advice or sympathy from a man who's pretty much said he won't ever give up *his* job to be a family man."

"I never said that. I said I love my job—"

"Yeah, well, my dad said that every time he headed out the door. I think you're the same way."

He didn't want to tell her she was in serious denial, about her dad, about him and about her own need to be loved. She wouldn't listen to that right now.

"I'm sorry," he replied. "I didn't mean to be so down on you or your family. It's none of my business, anyway."

"You're right, it's not." She motioned toward the clearing ahead of them. "The new pen area is around that bend. We've dug a pond and cemented the sides. Part of the chain-link fencing is up—or it was until someone messed with it. The landscaper should be out this week to place the sunning rocks and shade trees as well as the rest of the landscaping."

And just like that, she shifted gears away from her personal life to her work, showing Anderson that she depended on her work here to help her hide the pain of being abandoned by everyone she loved.

While he couldn't grasp the cruelty of that twist of fate, he could continue to help her and protect her. And he began to understand that while this case had brought him here, God had sent him here for more than just busting up a drug ring. He needed to help Jennifer Rodgers find her faith again. He prayed to the good Lord he could complete that task.

"Impressive setup," Anderson said, turning to Jennifer with a nod after they'd tethered the horses on some nearby bramble. He tried to avoid looking at her, but she saw the apology in his eyes.

Jennifer managed a smile, her regret at snapping at him making her think she was a lot like that tricky gator Bobby Wayne. She'd been nervous on the ride out here and then she'd gotten mad over Anderson's shock at her dysfunctional family history. It was something she didn't like to talk about, not even with her closest friends. And especially not with such a strong upstanding family man like Anderson Michaels. She envied him even while she wanted to hear all of his growing-up stories.

But Jennifer hid all of those conflicting needs behind a long sigh, taking her time to glance over the golden and mauve woods around them. The fall leaves were brilliant with colors that even her numb, shocked mind couldn't miss.

"It's supposed to be impressive and safe and secure," she replied. "I want to protect my alligators and also teach children about protecting wildlife. We'll put a few water turtles in here, too, but in another fenced area away from the gators. That's what that pile of rocks is for, to secure the fence line so the turtles won't escape. And I expect some of the native animals to wander in—at their own peril, of course."

She ventured a glance toward him. "I'm sorry I lost it back there. I get kind of touchy when it comes to my parents."

He shrugged, his boot hitting at a clump of clay. "I'm the one who should apologize. It's not my place to judge you, Jennifer. I'm just here to fight the bad guys and keep you safe." He glanced around, then lowered his voice. "And I have to remember you're still grieving for your father. This is a lot for you to take in—me being in your life all of a sudden like this."

"I can handle you, Ranger-man." She let it go at that

for now, since she didn't have a choice and since she was pretty sure she couldn't really handle him. "Okay, then. Truce. Let's look at the damaged fence."

He put his hands on his hips and nodded. "I saw lots of tracks when I went over it last night, but I'm guessing that's from construction workers coming and going."

"Yes, they've been bringing in backhoes and bulldozers for weeks now. And the big trucks bring in rocks and lumber for the feed house and the walls around the pond. We'll have plants delivered this week, probably. We have to work around the weather but we really need to get this done before winter sets in."

"Do alligators hibernate in winter?"

Glad to be back on a subject she could discuss, Jennifer bobbed her head. "They do if the temperatures go down too low. They're cold-blooded so they can't tolerate frigid temperatures. If they eat something and go into hibernation it can actually go bad inside their stomachs—not so good."

"How do you manage them?" he asked, his gaze moving around the muddy beginnings of the pond. "You don't actually go in the water with them, right?"

Jennifer laughed at that. "Of course not. But when I was little, my daddy taught me how to wrestle small alligators and crocodiles. It's not that hard if you stay calm and stay on their back side. But they are very sensitive to any type of vibration or movement on or near the water. And they can move quickly when provoked or surprised."

"I don't intend to find out," he retorted. He surveyed the lot again. "Looks like a definite trail through here. And it runs right toward where the new pond begins."

She moved around the oval-shaped pond, walking toward the spot where the old trail ended. "Yeah. Jacob commented on that last time the boys came back here with the four-wheelers." She pointed to the jagged tears in the tall chain-link fence. "They cut it down right there near the back part of the pond."

Anderson went to the torn fence and looked it over, then kicked at the ground and bent to pick up rocks and broken twigs. "It's hard to say who's been here. What with the construction people and the joyriders, it'll be nearly impossible to pinpoint exactly where the cartel has been doing the drops." He stood up and surveyed the nearby woods. "Why would they mess with your fence?"

"Maybe they don't even come on to my land," Jennifer replied, hoping against hope that would turn out to be the case. "It could have been Mr. Chason, like you said."

Anderson pointed toward the trailhead a few yards away. "Let's investigate over there near the tree line. I didn't go that far last night in case someone was lurking back there."

She followed him to where the worn path turned toward a curve. "Anderson, look."

Anderson hurried over to where an obvious campsite had been set up. "Those ashes look fresh. So that means someone was here after the last rain." Then he bent down and pointed to an object in the fire. "What's that?"

Jennifer stared down at the silver panel box. "That's the circuit board we ordered for the equipment house." She whirled to where a small shed sat off from the pond, outside of the protective fence. "They must have messed with the electrical system."

Anderson got up and rushed to the little house, then looked inside. "They've cut all the wiring."

"That means they've been back since we found the cut fence," Jennifer replied, a look of dismay on her face. "And you didn't see anything last night?"

"No, but it was dark and I stayed hidden out away from the site. I didn't want to shine any lights up here in case they were back. I didn't hear anything, either. They must have set this fire before I arrived on your property yesterday."

Jennifer gasped. "The construction crew had a controlled burn day before yesterday, late in the afternoon. Some trees and shrubs. But they made sure they'd put it out before they left for the day."

"The cartel could have come in later that night and used the original fire for a cover." He jotted notes. "So we have a fresh campfire and a damaged circuit breaker and cut wiring. They've sent a message and now they're laying low, which is why I didn't see anything last night. This place is too hot for them to have much activity. But since you have stirred things up, they could be gunning for you now. Which means I'm gunning for them. If they come back tonight, I'll be ready for them."

"Did you bring a tent to sleep in?"

"In my truck. But I'll use a bedroll. And I won't sleep."

Jennifer thought about that. "We could both hang out back here." At his inquisitive look, she added, "I'd bring my own tent, of course. And my Remington."

He shook his head, frowning at her. "You don't need

to do that. But I don't like leaving you all alone at your house, either."

"Anderson, I've been alone there off and on for years. My mother would come and go, then take off at a moment's notice and stay gone for months. Just like she did after my daddy died. I'm used to being alone."

"Things have changed, remember."

She pointed at the ruined circuit board, then stared at the open shed. "How can I forget?"

"Maybe I can rig some sort of security system back here, one that we can turn on at night that would alert both of us."

"You can do that?"

"I'll figure out something. Might be wise for you to have one anyway until the pen's security system is up and running. We'd keep it turned off during the day so the construction workers could come and go. But once they're gone for the day, we'd activate it."

Throwing up her hands, she said, "So what now? I mean what do we do until I get all that figured out?"

"I told you, I'll continue my stakeout back here. Sooner or later, they'll make another move."

She didn't want to think about that. But the man knew his job and she couldn't stop him from doing that job. Missing the old days when she was as free as a bird and glad to get home to a good movie or have a night out every now and then with her friends, she stared over at Anderson. The man was easy on the eyes and easy to get used to, even if he was so thorough and intense, he got on her nerves at times. But right now, she was just glad he was here.

Shaken by the damage and the cost of replacing her

fence and her electrical circuit, she stalked toward the campfire, then whirled to stare at him.

"What?" he asked, lifting his head toward her. "You find something else?"

"No." She glanced around again and spotted what looked like a cigarette butt on the ground a few feet from the ashes. Walking over the crusty dirt and grass, she leaned down to stare at it. "Anderson, I think I've found a…cigarette or something."

Anderson came over and bent to stare at the dirty white butt. "Yep. Looks like what's left of a joint. Not your average smoke."

"Marijuana? Pot on my property? I guess the drug runners stood around and got high while they watched my costly equipment burning to a crisp."

He pulled a set of plastic gloves out of his jacket pocket. "I don't doubt that. Unless this was left by Jacob and his friends or your rowdy neighbor."

"You really do suspect everyone, don't you?"

"Yep." He stood up and told her he'd be right back. She watched as he walked to Chestnut and dug into his saddle bag. When he returned with a saddle blanket and a black canvas bag, she guessed it was an evidence kit since he pulled out a tiny envelope and opened it wide. Reaching down with a pair of tweezers, he picked up the cigarette butt and dropped it in the bag, then sealed it and wrote on the outside. Then he pulled the circuit board out of the fire and carefully wrapped the blanket around the damaged board.

"Until I figure this thing out, everyone could be a suspect. Jacob mentioned your neighbor had run them off from here. He either wasn't at home earlier or he's avoiding people for some reason. I intend to pin him down, however."

"Good luck with that. The man *is* mean. He won't talk to me at all. I've tried calling him to explain why I need this new pond, but he hangs up on me."

"Remind me of what he said to you again."

"Other than the usual 'you'll regret this' type stuff, he's mostly a lot of hot air, I think."

"Maybe he *was* the one who ransacked your tack room."

"But why?"

"Just like you said before—to mess with you, maybe try to find some incriminating information regarding permits or animal cruelty or something."

"I've got all the permits in order and I'm not cruel to any of my animals."

"You can't be too careful. A threat is a threat and it should be treated as such, no matter what. Understand?"

She turned toward the horses. "I'm so tired of hearing that."

Anderson whirled her around so quickly, she felt the rush of air passing over her face.

"Jennifer, this isn't a joke. It's real."

She looked down at his fingers on her jacket, then back up to him, seeing the dark concern in his cat-like eyes. "I know that. That doesn't mean I have to like it." Then she slumped into a shrug. "You're scaring me, Anderson. And I've never been scared before. I've never worried about living here by myself or getting up in the middle of the night to check on a sick animal. I've taken long walks back here by myself many times, even before I bought the property. And to think I've allowed those teens back here when they could have been hurt or worse."

Stomping her feet to clear her boots of mud, she lifted a hand in the air then turned back toward the horses. "Now, everywhere I look, I feel as if someone is looking back at me through the trees, or lurking behind my stables just waiting to jump out at me. So give me some time to get used to all of this, okay?"

"Okay. Let's get back home."

They walked back around the pond to the horses.

Untying Sadie's rein and handing it to Jennifer, he said, "I get so caught up in the facts, I forget the reality of things like this. I understand this is hard to swallow and I get that you're used to being on your own and doing things your own way. But I took on this assignment for many reasons, one now being that I need to protect you whether you like it or not."

She got up on Sadie and stared down at him, her heart doing a strange little dance at that *worrying about her* part. And because she felt so guilty at being a whiny woman, she said, "Thank you. It's been a long time since anyone has bothered to worry about me."

Then she took off, leaving him sitting there on a stomping horse because she was too afraid to look back to see if he was following her.

SIX

"Anderson, come on in."

Captain Ben Fritz motioned as the Rangers gathered around the big conference table. Everybody in Company D wanted to catch the person who'd murdered Gregory Pike, so these weekly meetings had become mandatory. Anderson walked in and put his files down, then shook hands with Rangers Cade Jarvis and Oliver Drew.

Lieutenant Daniel Boone Riley motioned him over. "Hear we got a threat regarding the Alamo anniversary celebration."

Anderson nodded. "Yep, Ben updated me a few minutes ago. Let me get a better handle on this drop site and you and I can go to the meeting next week and have a talk with the planning committee. This is a big deal—the 175th anniversary of the Battle of the Alamo."

"I'll be ready," Daniel replied before taking his seat. "Meantime, I'll see what I can dig up regarding the threat."

After Rangers Gisella Hernandez, Levi McDonnell and several others entered the room, Ben gave a brief update, then turned things over to Anderson. "Tell us what you have so far."

Anderson stretched, trying to get the kinks out of his back. He'd headed straight to the bunkhouse yesterday after the ride out to the construction site, then back to the pond for the rest of the night, trying hard to focus on his job instead of Jennifer Rodgers.

Since Jennifer had left him in the dust after their exploration of the new alligator pond, he'd made sure she was safe inside the big house before he'd made himself a sandwich from the supplies she'd left for him, walked around the perimeter of the property, done a little paperwork and finally gone out to settle down out under the stars in his bedroll.

"Nobody visited the site during the wee hours last night," he said now. "I was awake back there most of the night—just me and a few coyotes and foxes, I think."

"Have to watch those foxes," Oliver said with a grin.

"Don't I know it," Anderson retorted. He went over a list of suggestions about the security around the rescue center.

And he had a list of reasons why he shouldn't be so attracted to Jennifer Rodgers, but he kept that list to himself. Ben would yank him right off this case if he even hinted at that attraction.

"Anderson?" Ben asked, jarring him back to business. "Got anything else to report?"

Anderson let out a grunt. "Miss Rodgers and I rode out to the alleged drop site yesterday to check on a new fence that was vandalized. It was cut with heavy-duty wire cutters. We also found a campsite that shows recent activity. And someone had deliberately dropped a brand-new circuit board into that campfire. They cut the power to her equipment and pumping shed, too. She had a small office and a refrigerator in there."

"You don't say." Ben let out a grunt. "The cartel's already harassing her?"

"Looks that way. She started construction on this new alligator pen last week. Somebody doesn't want any activity back there."

"Except the criminal kind," Cade retorted. "Anything else?"

"Miss Rodgers spotted what looks like part of a marijuana cigarette. Apparently, whoever this is has been taking time to smoke a little pot back there. I've tagged it for evidence and I'll get it to the crime lab along with everything else I have after I leave here. It's a long shot, but maybe the DNA will give us a hit."

Ben pushed at his chair. "That's a full report, Ranger."

"You're telling me," Anderson said. "Oh, and then there's the break-in at the tack room that I reported yesterday. But the place was pretty quiet last night. Haven't heard back from the lab on the prints I scanned from the barn incident, but honestly, I don't think we'll be able to get any prints on that. And she didn't get a good look at the man she saw running away from the cut fence."

"You think it's the ornery neighbor you mentioned?" Oliver asked as he jotted notes.

"My gut is leaning toward him. I can't see what a cartel lowlife would be doing snooping in there now that their man snitched to us, unless they hoped to scare Jennifer even more. I figure the cartel will keep coming if they think she knows something. I expect things to escalate if she refuses to stop building that pen."

"Just stay on top of things," Ben replied. "And remember, I'm assigning you and Daniel to sit in on the upcoming Alamo Planning Committee."

Daniel Riley lifted his head. "I'm happy to take the lead. We'll need to go over security measures since they received that cryptic letter."

Anderson nodded and wrote in his notebook. "Got it. That should be routine just as a precaution, right?"

"Should be," Ben said. "But these days, you never know. The letter indicated something bad would happen if the thing wasn't called off. I'll let you read the whole thing after the meeting."

Anderson didn't really savor sitting in on a boring committee meeting, but the 175th Anniversary of the Battle of the Alamo coming up this summer was a big deal around here. Threatening letters regarding a celebration with a big crowd of people couldn't be good—whether serious or not.

"Okay. We'll check into it." He looked over his notes. "Regarding this case, I'll keep trying to make contact with that disgruntled neighbor I told you about—Ralph Chason. He didn't answer his door and I saw no sign of him around his property. I'm running a check on him."

"Just keep at it," Ben said, glancing around. "By the way, our coma man hasn't moved a muscle and the photo's been on all the news stations and in the papers for at least a couple of days. If we get any hits on that, Anderson, you'll need to be in on the action. I'd like you to follow through on any leads."

"I can do that," Anderson replied, glad to have something to focus on. "It's slow-going around the farm. But hey, I'm learning how to feed hawks and milk goats. And I never knew there were so many kinds of turtles in this world."

Gisella chuckled. "And how are the alligators?"

Anderson let out a laugh. "So far, so good. I tend to stay away from them. The new pen is definitely infringing on the drug cartel's territory. Looks like an old trail runs right through one side of the land being turned into the gator park."

Oliver shot him a glance. "They might stay away if they think it's too hot."

"Not if they've already starting wreaking havoc on Jennifer's plans. I guess they think she'll shut it down if they harass her. So far, they've only damaged property but the threats could get more personal."

"Yeah, and that's where you come in, my friend," Ben reminded him. "Stay on the case, but watch out for Miss Rodgers, too."

The group compared notes for a while longer, then the meeting was dismissed. Anderson looked around as the others left the room, thinking he'd lay down his life for any one of them. This was a strong team. But this kind of work was hard on any sort of home life. They all tended to stay away from serious relationships because of that very reason.

He was a Ranger first, Anderson thought on the drive back to the rescue farm. His job was harsh and hard and time-consuming. In his mind, that left very little room for a normal life. He knew not to mix business with pleasure.

So why did Jennifer make him dream of things he'd vowed to not think about? Such as romantic dinners, long walks in a meadow, maybe a boat ride on the river? He'd never had much time for anything other than the occasional hunting trip with his father and brothers. He never had time to date. Best he remember that and focus on the job, rather than the woman he was getting to know.

He parked and glanced around once he'd entered the gates. Everything looked perfectly normal. No one would ever suspect some dangerous criminals might be doing their nocturnal dirty work around here.

Anderson went inside the bunkhouse, leaving the door open to the cool air, then put on a pot of coffee to percolate. He decided to call Ben.

"I thought of something else. Might as well run a check on the part-time helper—Jacob Slaton. I think he's clean but...you never know. He's worked here for a few years now and seems like a good kid." He gave Ben all the information he'd managed to glean from talking to both Jacob and Jennifer.

When he turned back toward the door, he found Jennifer standing there with a basket of what looked like muffins. But before he could grab at one of the good-smelling muffins, she sat the basket down with a heavy thud, causing the contents to bounce up and down.

"You're doing a check on Jacob?"

"Oh, you heard that?"

"Yes, I heard that," she retorted, her eyes full of anger and accusation. "Honestly, why don't you just arrest the both of us and shut the place down since you don't trust anyone around here."

"Hey," he said, his own frustrations matching hers, "I told you everyone is suspect. I thought we'd gotten past this, Jennifer. I'm also getting background information on your neighbor Ralph Chason, too."

She frowned, tapped her booted foot, frowned some more, then finally let out a long sigh. "I don't like it, but I guess I understand. I came here to share these as a peace offering." Shoving the muffins at him, she said, "Here. One of our volunteers brought 'em by. She's in the goat pen right now. You might want to frisk her and run a check on her, too. But I can give you a physical description. She's almost five feet tall with gray hair and she's usually wearing some sort of velour and good quality orthopedic shoes. Real dangerous-looking granny."

Anderson had to put his hand over his mouth to keep from laughing. "I'll get right on that."

She held a mock frown. "I just reckon you will."

Jennifer plopped down on a rickety high-backed chair. "Her name is Ethel and she plays the organ at the local church. That is, when she's not hanging around the campfire waiting for the next drug runner to appear."

He sniffed at the muffins and picked one up. "I get the picture. I might have to question her, but I promise I won't frisk her."

Waiting for her to smile, he motioned toward the old percolator he'd found in the tiny efficiency kitchen. "I found the supplies and food staples you left—thanks for that. It looks like mud, but I made coffee. Want some?"

She shook her head. "I just drank my quota for the day. I didn't sleep very well." Her look indicated his presence and the problems with her gator pond were the reasons. But she reached for a muffin. "Do you ever get tired of tracking down criminals?"

Anderson poured himself a cup of the rich brew then sat down across from her. "I get physically tired and I get aggravated as all get-out, but no, I don't get tired of bringing criminals to justice. It's my life."

She let that soak in. "Well, you'll never run out of them, that's for sure."

Anderson bit into the juicy muffin. "Hmm. That is good. I think I need to meet Miss Ethel."

Jennifer finally laughed and ate her own muffin. "She'll fall for you right away. She might be old and a widow but she likes to flirt." She leaned close. "Especially with a tall, handsome Ranger."

Anderson leaned in, too, giving her a playful smile. "Is that how *you* see me?"

She immediately stood up, her blush as pretty as a new blooming rose. "I'm not sure how I see you—except as someone who's here to remind me I'm no longer safe in my own home. I gotta go call the electrician and make up some explanation as to why my circuit box got toasted. Just wanted to give you a muffin."

He noted the worry in her eyes, then grabbed another muffin, deciding he wouldn't push the issue for now. "Thanks. I'll be out to help with the rest of the morning feedings in a few minutes."

She backed toward the door, then glanced up at him. "So did you stay up all night filing your reports and running background checks on people? Or did you do the stakeout thing all night?"

"How do you know I was up last night?"

She blushed again. He sure loved that sweet blush. "I told you…uh…I couldn't sleep, so I roamed the house and saw your light on around midnight."

He didn't tell her that he left the light on for a reason. "I spent most of the night out on my stakeout."

Her brows lifted at that. "And?"

"Nothing. All quiet for now."

"I kept waking up, thinking about someone deliberately cutting that fence and frying that circuit breaker. I don't like feeling so vulnerable. It's creepy."

It would be hard to sleep knowing everything you held dear was being threatened. "I'm doing everything I can to nip this in the bud, Jennifer. Just bear with me."

"Easy for you to say. It's like waiting for a lion to pounce."

She had no idea her choice of words hit the nail on the head. "I won't let any lions get you," he said, allowing her a long look.

She nodded on that. "I think I could handle a real lion better than a threat I can't see."

"I hear you. Hey, about the construction crew coming in—let's stick with the cover of me just being a new hire. We can't be certain one of them isn't involved in this mess."

"Great. Now I have that angle to consider, too."

He followed her outside. It was turning out to be a nice fall day—crisp and cool with just a hint of winter in the wind.

"There's always an angle to consider," he said. He

couldn't tell her a lot about this case. But he could keep reminding her that she was in danger.

She whirled to stare up at him. "What happens if *nothing* happens, Anderson? How long can you stay here?"

"Until I find something," he replied. "I'm gonna bunk down near the alligator pen every night." Then he pointed to a big sack on the table. "First, I'm gonna make this place a little more secure."

"I told you, I can't afford a security system right now. I have lights and cameras ready to be hooked up, but they're not working yet."

"I'll improvise," he replied. "Don't worry about it."

She stomped her boots. "I don't have time to worry about it. I'm going to check on Ethel and the goats."

"Okay. I'll finish up in here and find you. Then I'll sweet-talk Ethel into staying here with you a bit longer so I can track down Ralph Chason."

"I don't need a babysitter."

"I didn't say that. I don't want you alone right now."

"As if Ethel could save me."

"You said yourself she has sturdy orthopedic shoes."

She shot him another raised-eyebrow glance. "Well, she did use to be a marathon runner. And she knows how to use a shotgun."

"There you go, then."

He watched her prance away, the mental image of Jennifer in a pretty dress by his side while they strolled along the Riverwalk causing him to shake his head. "Whoa, there, Anderson. No time for that kind of day-dreaming."

And yet, he couldn't get that image out of his mind. Maybe he should eat another muffin and be done with it.

"Another day, another dollar," Jennifer told Jacob later as they finished up for the day. All the animals had been fed and watered as usual. They rotated cleaning the cages on a daily basis and today's cleanings had gone off without too much trouble—no animals escaping or getting ornery with them. Her favorites, the turtles, seemed to be thriving, too. Very important since hunters could get a non-game permit to capture turtles and export them to other countries as a delicacy. Jennifer rescued a lot of turtles from too-cold waters or from storms tossing them into shallow waters. That's how she'd found her very first turtle when she was young.

Remembering how gentle her father had been with the almost hypothermic creature they'd found in a shallow wash on Padre Island one brutal winter, Jennifer closed her eyes to the grief forming inside her soul. Her father had practically brought the comatose turtle back to life. So why had he let himself go and get killed in a boat that had flipped over into snake-infested waters?

Because Martin Rodgers had lived for the thrill and the danger of his job. Same with Anderson Michaels. Anderson might not look for wild animals, but he did look for unscrupulous criminals. Did he live for the thrill and the danger of his job? Did he find it easy to walk away from any kind of intimate commitment?

She should keep her mind on her turtles and not Ranger-man, Jennifer thought as she quickly opened her eyes to reality. Anderson wouldn't stay around. He'd go back to his own life once this case was over and solved.

But her immediate concern still involved him. Anderson had been gone for over two hours. He was out there somewhere, trying to find a disgruntled neighbor. What if the neighbor had found him first?

Jennifer had enjoyed the freedom earlier, glad that he wasn't underfoot or front and center in her mind for a change. Jacob had come after school to help out and Ethel had stayed to lend a hand. She was in the front office right now, explaining to some tourist about the renovations and apologizing because they couldn't take a stroll around the entire property. And if Jennifer knew Ethel, she'd also give them a discount pass for the grand reopening next spring. They needed to keep visitors aware.

Ethel had stayed, all right, after meeting Anderson and preening like a swan right in front of the man.

"A tall drink of water, that one," Ethel had whispered after Anderson headed out the open gate to the highway. "Where on earth did you find him, Jennifer?"

"He kind of wandered up," Jennifer had told her older friend, amused at Ethel's silly smiles and big, curious eyes. "He's here to help with the new pen. You know, making sure the security measures are up to snuff." It wasn't the whole truth, but Ethel *had* been warned of the problems back there.

"Are you gonna try to train him?"

Laughing, Jennifer had shaken her head. "I don't think Anderson can be trained, Miss Ethel. He's just here for a few weeks."

She hoped. She prayed. And she hoped shrewd Ethel

would buy that story. Jennifer didn't need matchmaking on top of all her other worries.

"Well, it'd sure be a shame to let him slip away," Ethel had replied in her soft, sweet voice. "If I was about thirty years younger—"

"Miss Ethel," Jennifer had said, feigning shock. Then she'd sighed. "I do have to agree with you but—"

"You need to find a good man," Ethel replied with an endearing smile. "That's the best kind of security."

Jennifer didn't have the heart to tell her friend that finding a man did not necessarily mean instant security. Her mother never had that luxury. And she needed to remember that, no matter how much Anderson promised her he'd be around to help her. Jennifer wanted to believe in a forever kind of love, but she was afraid to think in those terms. Anderson Michaels was a prime example of a man who'd rather get up and go to work than deal with a woman in his life. Or so she imagined.

"You don't have to stay," Jennifer had said, hoping Ethel would take the hint. "We're wrapping things up."

Ethel had left the subject of Jennifer's single status alone. "Oh, but I don't mind a bit. Anderson wanted me to help you label the feed buckets and man the front office, since he had to run those important errands. He seems good at organizing things."

"Oh, yeah. He's been a great help to me."

And a hindrance, a distraction, an annoyance.

But she missed him—and he'd only been gone two hours. And that made her angry at herself and even angrier at Anderson. She didn't want to miss him or care about him or even like him, for that matter. She barely knew the man so why the sudden interest? She told herself she didn't care.

But she did.

She looked over at Jacob and said, "You can go. Take off a little early. I'll go inside with Ethel and help her shut down the office."

"Thanks," Jacob said, spinning on his sneakers. Then he turned around to stare over at her. "Hey, Jennifer, is everything all right around here?"

"What do you mean?"

"That Anderson dude. He seems okay but…he keeps asking me a lot of questions. Have I done something wrong?"

Grrr. "No, you haven't done anything wrong. It's kind of complicated, but he's just here to beef up the security down at the new pond since we've had some vandalism back there. He won't be around very long. And, Jacob, we don't need to broadcast that he's here, okay?"

"Oh, all right. I'll see you tomorrow, then."

Jacob didn't seem convinced but what else could she say to the kid? *Hey, Jacob, by the way, we might have drug runners on that spot near the new alligator pen.*

Jacob waved goodbye and hopped in his truck.

Jennifer looked forward to going inside with Ethel. She'd make a nice pot of tea and share one last muffin with her friend.

Then she heard Chestnut's high-pitched whinnying and turned toward the stables. Dusk was settling in and the day was turning cold. Shivering, Jennifer called out as she ran down the lane and entered the stables. "Chestnut, you don't need another treat—"

A shadow hovered at the far end of the old barn.

And she was pretty sure it wasn't Ethel standing there. But it was human.

"Anderson?" she called out, thinking maybe he'd come home without her noticing.

No response.

"Who's there?"

Chestnut whinnied again, then began stomping his hooves against the stall. Jennifer didn't need any further warning. If her horse sensed danger then she'd take that as the gospel.

She turned to leave, her legs shaking. But she didn't want to leave her animals in there, either. She whirled, glancing around for some sort of protection.

And that's when she heard footsteps hurry toward her.

SEVEN

Stumbling, Jennifer glanced around for help or a weapon. Jacob was gone and Ethel would never hear her screams. She'd have to either outrun her pursuer or stop and fight. But if she ran away, her animals might be in danger. Chestnut was in a frenzy already. The big horse could very easily break out of his stall.

She saw a jagged limb about the size of a baseball bat that the recent storm had dislodged from an ancient pine tree. Grabbing it up, she hopped around the side of the barn and waited, listening for more footsteps.

The old barn went silent. Deadly silent. Then she heard Chestnut snorting and kicking again.

Where did he go? she wondered, her breath held, her pulse jittery and wild. She could handle spooked animals but dealing with a dangerous human was another thing.

She moved an inch closer to the open doors, praying that whoever had been in there was now gone. But Chestnut's loud snorts indicated the gelding still wasn't happy.

Well, neither was she.

Turning, she decided she'd be better off backtracking

around the barn. She decided to sneak in the other way and try to find out if the intruder was still in there.

Taking slow, steady steps, Jennifer tried not to make any noise. But her boot on a fat twig caused an echoing crackle to fill the dusk.

Then she heard hurried footsteps again.

And they seemed to be getting closer.

Jennifer whirled at the back of the barn, the sturdy log raised like a giant sword. With a wham that was met with a thud, she managed to hit her target.

The man went down, but he got right back up. Jennifer screamed and swung again, too startled to get a good look at his face. But it wouldn't have mattered. He was wearing a loose hoodie that covered most of his features. Except his eyes. They glowed black and menacing against the darkness of the barn.

"Who arc you?" she shouted, praying Ethel would finally hear and call for help. And praying Ethel wouldn't take the law into her own hands and grab a weapon.

The man lunged toward Jennifer, but she pivoted away, grunting as she lifted the tree limb again. "Get off my propcrty!"

The man didn't speak but he came forward, prepared to charge her like a bull. Jennifer screamed again, bracing herself, the rough bark of the log scraping at her palms and arms as she tried to once again fend off her attacker.

The man overpowered her, grabbing at the log as he forced her to the ground. "You need to stop work on that gator pen, lady…permanently," he said on a hiss of air, his voice low and grainy, the smell of sweat and dirt surrounding him.

Jennifer had a quick glance of olive skin and a mustache. Then he sat back on his heels, lifted the log over his head and with a grunt, brought it down.

Jennifer screamed and rolled away, the thud of crashing wood next to her temple causing her to wrap her arms against her head and scream again.

Then she heard a gunshot. Daring to glimpse up, she looked around for her attacker. But he was gone.

Anderson's heart was caught somewhere between his ribs and his throat. Holding his Sig Sauer pistol out in a protective stance, he hurried around the barn. "Jennifer?"

"I'm here." She sounded weak and winded, but she was alive at least. He thanked God for that.

Rushing around the barn, he saw her there on the ground, sitting in a huddled ball.

"Are you all right?" he said as he stooped to help her up.

"Yes, go." She pointed toward the woods. "He went that way."

Anderson followed the direction she'd indicated. "I'll be right back." He ran toward the woods, crouching near the fence line. A gaping hole showed where the intruder had managed to crawl through. Anderson called 911, then hurried through the cut fence.

Only to find the woods empty. Should he go after the man or go back and check on Jennifer? It was growing dark and for all he knew the man might have circled back to finish the job. Anderson whirled and ran back to the barn.

"He's gone for now," he told Jennifer. "I've called 911. Let me see about you."

Holding his breath, he checked for wounds but didn't see any. Then he felt her palms and looked down. "You're all cut up. What happened?"

Jennifer gulped in a breath. "He came into the stables. Chestnut warned me—he was agitated. I came to investigate and saw a shadow. I grabbed that branch and came around the barn." She pointed down to where a broken pine tree limb lay. "I hit him once, I think."

Anderson glanced around to make sure the man wasn't back. "I heard you screaming the minute I got out of my truck. I don't think I hit him, but I must have scared him off. I couldn't get a clean shot."

"Is he really gone?" She twisted around to look into the growing dusk.

Anderson searched the trees and nearby woods. "I think so. He'd be crazy to hang around now." He took her under one arm, careful to hold his gun away. "Let's get you to the house."

"But the horses—"

"I'll come back and check on everything, I promise. I'll explain to the sheriff, too."

She nodded, allowing him to guide her up the lane. "Let me know if anything's wrong, okay?"

Frustrated with her one-track mind, Anderson said, "I understand, but...you're more important than the horses, Jennifer. Why didn't you run?"

"I tried. But I saw that big branch and thought I could wallop him. I wanted him to know I didn't appreciate being scared like that." She shuddered, then pushed at her disheveled hair. "He told me I'd better cancel plans for the alligator pen."

Anderson let that settle, then asked, "Did you get a good look at him?"

"Not really. He was wearing a hood I think and he had a mustache. Dark eyes. Olive skin from what I could tell. I was more intent on cracking his head open."

In spite of nearly having a heart attack, Anderson couldn't help the tight smile. "I think you must have given him a run for his money. He sure got out of here quick."

"Not me," she said, her nose against his chest. "You shot at him."

"Too bad I missed."

He'd definitely be bunking outside on his bedroll again tonight. The vandalism was bad enough. And now a solid verbal threat and physical attack. This was getting out of hand. What were they trying to protect back there?

Ethel met them on the porch. "I thought heard a gun-shot! And I hear sirens."

"It's okay," Jennifer said, lifting away from Anderson's embrace. Then she looked over at Anderson, doubt in her eyes.

Anderson took over. "Somebody messing in the barn. I heard Jennifer screaming and ran to help. I got a little trigger-happy, but they ran away."

Ethel held her hand to her heart. "Why would any-body do that?"

Anderson replied, trying to stay honest. "Someone's probably trespassing. He got too close."

"Goodness," Ethel said, taking Jennifer by the arm. "Honey, I've never seen you so flustered. Are you sure you're okay?"

"He kind of spooked me," Jennifer said on a breath. "It was so dark in the barn, and Chestnut was upset."

Ethel gave her a hug. "Bless your heart. You don't need this on top of all your other worries."

Jennifer cast a look toward Anderson. "I'm all right, really. Scared me more than I care to admit."

"I don't mind staying," Ethel said to Anderson.

"You can go on home," Anderson replied. "I'll make sure everything's okay. I'll check the barn again."

Ethel stood silent, taking in the scene, probably taking in Anderson's protective stance, too. Then she shrugged and whirled. "I think you're in good hands here, Jennifer, so I'll go. But you call me if you need anything, you hear?"

"I will," Jennifer said. "Thank you so much, Miss Ethel."

Anderson urged her inside. "I'll go talk to the sheriff's deputy." He walked Ethel to her car, thanked her and then hurried back to the barn. After searching every nook and cranny, he soothed Chestnut and the other horses with a treat, then came back inside to Jennifer.

She was sitting there, staring at her torn hands. His heart broke for her. She was a strong woman, a force to be reckoned with. She'd been brave to turn on her attacker tonight. Too brave.

"Where's your first aid kit?" he asked, storming around the kitchen, his mind whirling with the worst-case scenario of what could have happened in that barn.

"In the supply closet by the hall bathroom. Did you go back to the barn?"

"Yeah. Horses are secure and the barn is clear."

He found the kit and came back, then bent down in front of her. "This is gonna burn," he said after taking out the alcohol. Grabbing some cotton balls, he doused one. "Ready?"

She bobbed her head. "I can handle it."

He knew she could. But he tried to be gentle as he pressed the cotton ball against her torn flesh. She winced, then closed her eyes.

"I'm sorry," he said, watching as a single tear rolled down her left cheek. "I shouldn't have left you."

She opened her eyes and pulled back. "I can take care of myself. But I won't let anyone harm my animals."

"I get that," he replied, trying to choose the right words. "But…you're in real danger now and I'm here to help you. Only I don't seem to be doing a very good job."

"You did help me. You scared him away. So please don't apologize."

Anderson went back to ministering her wounds. "Let's put some of this antibiotic ointment on here, just in case."

She allowed him to dab some of the white cream across the scratches and cuts, gritting her teeth each time he touched a raw spot.

Anderson let his fingers linger on her skin too long, his awareness of her as overpowering as his need to protect her. "There, all done."

"Thanks," she said, her gaze locking with his before she looked down at her hands again.

Did she feel the same way?

He put away the supplies and dropped the cotton balls in the trash. Then he turned back to her and bent down in front of her. "Hungry?"

"No."

"Want some of that green tea? I can make it hot."

She nodded, her frown softer now as it turned into a silent pout.

Anderson wanted her to scream and fight with him, but she seemed to be shutting down, the last of her innocent assumptions that she would be all right disappearing in the cold night air. Thinking you were invincible could be a curse or a blessing, depending on the situation. Anderson figured Jennifer had inherited some of her rugged father's spunk and courage, but this kind of trouble could make or break that spirit.

He took her hands in his, careful not to press her wounds. "I'm sorry, Jennifer. For all of this."

She finally looked into his eyes, her expression bordering on frustration and acceptance. "I believe you. And I'm glad you're here. I wasn't so happy to see you at first. I thought you were just some hotshot lawman overreacting to a big case. I honestly didn't believe what you were telling me. I do now."

A strange feeling came over Anderson as he sat there, holding her hands in his, holding his gaze on her. And because that feeling was so new and electric, so surprising and so heated with a sweet rush of warmth, he did something he figured he'd regret later.

He leaned close and touched his lips to hers, slowly at first, and then with an intake of breath, he fell to his knees and pulled her down into his arms and kissed her good and proper.

And right now, he didn't regret it at all.

She would regret this later, Jennifer thought. She'd regret it when she couldn't sleep at three in the morning and she got up to find a light burning in the bunkhouse. She'd regret it tomorrow in the light of day when she had to look Anderson in the eye again.

She'd regret it later, but not now. Surely not right now when leaning into his arms was the balm she needed for her bruised heart and her still-racing pulse. So she gave in to Anderson's kiss, allowing herself this one temptation before reality set back in. And it would. She accepted that real life would come between them.

Maybe sooner than she thought.

He pulled away to stare up at her, the shimmering surprise in his eyes matching the erratic shock pouring through her system. "Wow."

Jennifer watched as he stood and ran a hand over his crisp hair. "Wow," he said again, spinning on his boots. "I'll make us some of that healthy tea."

And just like that, it was over. But then, none of this was really over yet. He wouldn't leave now and she couldn't let him leave now. Her life was forever changed by an intruder. Not only did she now need to fear for her life and guard herself against danger. Oh, no. Now she had to worry about another intruder.

One who was becoming dear to her in spite of her better judgment.

Anderson Michaels scared her just about as much as the attacker inside her barn.

So she was caught between a rock and a hard place, needing a man who'd walked larger than life right into her safe, routine world, and wishing she'd never met him even when she thanked God she had. She hadn't seriously prayed to God in a long time, but now she found herself not only thanking Him but asking Him to watch over Anderson. And her.

I don't deserve it, Lord. I don't deserve Your guiding hand since I haven't been faithful lately. But I'm asking now, for Anderson's sake. He truly is a good and faithful servant.

"We're in a fine mess here, Anderson," she said after her silent prayer, because facing the truth was much easier than ignoring it.

"I told you, I'll get these people, one way or another."

"I wasn't talking about the bad guys," she replied, standing, her gaze centered on him.

He whirled to stare over at her, his expression bordering on yet another apology. Instead, he surprised her. "I'm not sorry, Jennifer. Not about that kiss if that's what you're wondering. But...we both know it was wrong."

"Yeah, we both know that. Don't worry, Ranger-man. I'll try not to distract you from doing your job. Especially when that job involves protecting me."

"Too late on that, darlin'," he said with a faint grin. "You became a distraction the day I walked in this place. Nothing for it now, though. We finish this out. And I have a feeling your being a distraction is gonna get worse before it gets better."

Jennifer couldn't wait for the better part.

And by the way he was looking at her, she had the feeling he couldn't, either.

EIGHT

"Okay, you have my cell number," Anderson told Jennifer for the fifth time. "And your friend Becky is coming to stay the night with you, right?"

"Yes," Jennifer replied, trying not to lose her patience. He was covering all the bases. And yet her skin crawled at the thought of Anderson patrolling her property alone throughout the night. "I don't get why I can't come with you."

"We've been over this, Jennifer," he said, his eyes lighting up with a defiant fire. "I know how to handle this. And while you might be able to fire a weapon, it's just too dangerous for you right now."

"And I'm a distraction, right?" She didn't need him to spell that out to her after that kiss they'd had earlier.

He bent to give her a peck on the cheek. "Yes, ma'am, you are surely that. And I need you to promise me you won't do anything crazy like follow me. That's why I wanted your friend to come. I'm putting her in charge of making sure you don't leave the house tonight."

"I can outrun Becky," she said on a teasing note. But when she saw that Anderson-serious look, she bobbed her head. "Okay, all right. I'll be a good little girl and keep the doors locked. But I'm keeping my rifle close, too."

"That's better." He glanced at his watch. "Is Becky on her way?"

"Due any minute," Jennifer retorted. "She had to come through rush hour traffic from San Antonio, remember?"

"I'm just edgy," he admitted. "Ready to get on with things."

She could see the adrenaline pumping in the throbbing pulse lining his jaw. A flashback to her father stalking a rattlesnake caused her to remember that some men lived for the hunt, for the challenge. And because of that, those types of men could never really settle down.

Was Anderson that way? He did seem to thrive on his work. But…he'd also been kind to her. When she thought of how he'd doctored her wounds and then kissed her earlier, she felt ashamed that she'd compared him to her father. Her father had been a kind, good man but he'd also been willing to abandon his wife and child at a moment's notice for the call of adventure. In the end, he truly had abandoned both of them, even if her parents were divorced, by putting himself in enough danger to end his life.

And I haven't forgiven him yet for that, Jennifer thought now, an epiphany edging her mind. Was that why she'd stopped going to church? Was she angry at God as well as her earthly father?

Maybe that was why she'd decided Anderson wasn't the settling-down type, either. He'd hinted at that. His job demanded complete dedication. And he was honorable enough to recognize that.

"Hey, you gonna be all right?" Anderson asked, the look of concern in his eyes her undoing.

Pushing away the startling realization for now, she said, "I'll be fine, I promise. I won't try anything stupid. I want this over."

He leaned close, his gold-edged eyes shimmering in the lamplight. "Me, too. For a whole lot of reasons."

A knock at the kitchen door interrupted the moment.

"That must be Becky."

The look of regret he shot her told Jennifer it was a good thing they'd been interrupted.

She headed to the door and opened it wide to greet her friend. "Hey, Becky."

"Girl, what is going on?" Becky asked, sweeping in with a breezy smile, her energy bouncing off the walls. "I don't mind coming for a slumber party one bit since I have the next two days off, anyway, but you sounded so strange on the phone—" She stopped to look up at Anderson, a perky grin tipping her lips. "And I so want to hear all about this."

Jennifer remembered what Anderson had told her. She had to be careful in what information she gave out to her friends and coworkers. "It's nothing, really. Just some vandalism and a trespasser in the barn. My new worker Anderson offered to patrol the place tonight to see if he can catch anyone. He's helping with the security."

Becky looked Anderson up and down. "Did you call the police? And when did you hire a new worker?"

"I hired him this week," Jennifer replied. "And we

called the sheriff. Anderson talked to him and seems to think we can handle it."

Anderson nodded. "It's nice to meet you, Becky. And thanks for coming out. If I see anything out of the ordinary, I'll call in reinforcements."

"Wait," petite, red-headed Becky said, running a hand through her short, shagged hair. "You *are* a cop, aren't you?"

"What makes you think that?" Jennifer asked, shooting her friend a warning look.

Becky grinned again. "I work at the Bexar County Courthouse, remember? I see his type coming and going all day long." She waved a hand toward Anderson. "He's in lock and load mode, all right."

Anderson let out a grunt, his expression resolved. "I'm a security expert," he said. "But you can't reveal that to anyone, you understand? It could be dangerous for both Jennifer and you. And since I now know you work at the courthouse…"

Becky lifted her head back. "Wow, I get it, already. Whatever's going on, I'm here for the night and I know nothing." Then she pointed a finger at him. "But I don't like being threatened."

"I'm not a threat to you," Anderson replied, clearly in charge in spite of Becky's bravado. "Just explaining how it has to be, okay?"

"Okay." Becky looked around. "I need a drink of water."

Jennifer watched her friend head to the refrigerator, then glared at Anderson. "Thanks for scaring her, too."

"I'm not trying to scare anyone," he said on a tired

breath. "She guessed things. I verified things. And I told her how things are. That's it. And now, I'm going out there to ride the property. I won't be back until the sun comes up."

Jennifer prayed he would come back, even if he did infuriate her at times with that firm stance. "Be careful."

He nodded, then turned to Becky. "Sorry if I seemed harsh with you. I was just surprised you figured me out so quickly."

Becky took a swig of her water. "Hey, I see a lot of law enforcement people coming and going at work, and you fit the bill perfectly. It might be your place to get to the bottom of this vandalism deal, but it's my place to watch Jennifer's back, got it?"

"Got it," he said as he turned at the door. "And I wouldn't have it any other way. But you have to abide by my request, okay?"

"Since you asked so nice, okay," Becky said with a wry grin.

Jennifer watched him leave, then turned to find Becky staring at her with bright green eyes. "Okay, time to spill it, girl. And I mean, I want all the details. How'd you get so lucky to have a good-looking 'security expert' at your beck and call?" She pushed a finger at Jennifer's arm. "They only bring in Rangers on the big stuff, know what I mean?"

Anderson rubbed Chestnut's neck then spoke softly to the big gelding. "Thanks for coming with me, boy. You're a good, strong trooper."

The horse snorted and trotted along the fence line,

up for a run in spite of the cold night air. Anderson had to admit he needed some fresh air himself. He had a lot to think over. Mainly, why had he gone and kissed Jennifer?

And how could he keep from kissing her again?

Was it wrong, Lord? Should I ignore these strange, exciting feelings I get every time I look at the woman? Or should I accept that maybe, like my mama's always said, my tune is changing?

Was this his time, Anderson wondered while he checked the fence, looked for any signs of activity, and prayed to the Lord to show him the way on this. Being around Jennifer sure felt right. And he could show her she could trust him and trust in the Lord to see her through. Anderson knew he had a purpose here—to get the bad guys. That was his job and he lived and breathed his job. He'd never much thought about settling down. But maybe God had another purpose in mind for him. To get Jennifer back into the Father's loving arms.

"And I wouldn't mind one bit if she'd fall into my arms now and then," he said on a whisper. Then he did a mental shakedown. That couldn't happen until this case was over.

He reached the new alligator pond. The place was shadowy in spite of the full moon overhead. While the gators were still safe in their old pen, this new one would be better all the way around. The alligators would be contained and so would any humans coming to view them. Jennifer had been smart to rebuild. That is, until she'd gotten in the way of the cartel.

He edged his way around the chain-link fence, noting the gaping tear. Dismounting, he tethered Chestnut on the gate and walked the perimeter of the pond, checking for any new footprints. Had the cartel moved things up a notch by trying to attack Jennifer? They kept coming back here for a reason. Hidden drugs, maybe? Or worse?

Who had been in Jennifer's barn today? And why?

He'd sent what little evidence they'd found to the state lab. His fellow Ranger Cade Jarvis would give him an update on that soon. Maybe they'd get a hit from the DNA on that joint.

Anderson carefully made his way to the campsite, taking in the ashes and burnt pieces of wood. Nothing new there. Would the cartel strike again tonight?

He stood still, listening to the night sounds. Off in the distance a coyote howled, adding to the eeriness of the moon's midnight glow. The wind picked up, rattling leaves from the nearby trees. Chestnut snorted, skittish in spite of his bravery.

Anderson wished he had a good feeling about this. It was too quiet back here. He went over what he knew just to keep from jumping out of his skin. The fence and electrical wiring had been cut, the circuit breaker destroyed. The tack room had been searched and ransacked and an intruder had come into the barn, apparently bent on hurting Jennifer. The man had told her to stop the work back here.

They had an ornery noncommunicative neighbor fighting against the new alligator pen. That same neighbor had warned Jacob and his friends to stay away from this part of Jennifer's property. Did the man just want some peace and quiet or did *he* have a hidden agenda?

Anderson would have to get to the bottom of that.

First thing in the morning, he'd finish getting the security measures in place and then he'd go back to talk to Ralph Chason. If he could find the man.

Since everything seemed quiet, Anderson got his bedroll and settled down, Chestnut standing nearby to keep him company while his Remington shotgun kept him secure. Since he couldn't sleep, he said a prayer for Jennifer to stay secure, too. He lay still, looking around. Then he sat straight up. The security cameras! They weren't on, but what if somebody thought they were? And what if that someone thought Jennifer had his face on video?

"Oh, that was such a good movie," Becky said. Passing the last of the popcorn toward Jennifer, she grinned. "Don't you love a happy ending?"

Jennifer didn't want to burst her ever-positive friend's bubble but she didn't believe in happy endings. "It's easy to make that happen in a movie. Not always the case in real life."

"Your attitude is lacking," Becky said with a kick of her bright green fuzzy ankle boots. The boots matched her green-and-blue-striped flannel pajamas. "You have to believe in love, Jennifer."

Jennifer pulled her plush blue turtle-embossed robe close then stared at her friend. "I try. In fact, I kind of had a lightbulb moment tonight before you got here. I think I've been staying away from church and my faith because…I'm angry at my dad for dying. Is that too weird?"

Becky's green eyes brightened. "Not so weird. It's easy to blame God when we lose a loved one. But you do need to forgive your daddy. The man didn't plan to die, you know."

"But he did plan that trip even though he knew it could be very dangerous. My mother even begged him not to go. She still loved him."

"That was his life, Jen. He loved his work."

Jennifer started picking up their dishes. "And that's the point. He loved his work more than anything else. Even me."

Becky followed her into the kitchen. "He loved you. You know that. He took you with him on some of his trips."

Jennifer stood at the window, staring out into the shadows of the night. "He did teach me everything about animals and yes, I love my work here as much as he loved his. But…I don't know if I'd put work ahead of family."

Becky came to stand beside her. "But aren't you doing that very thing? You rarely leave this place. And now you have a handsome Ranger willing to help you stay safe, but from what you've told me, you haven't so much as batted an eye at the man."

Jennifer hadn't told her friend about the kiss. That was too new and unexpected and confusing to share, even with her best friend. "I just met Anderson a few days ago. That's probably why he hasn't proposed yet," she said with dripping sarcasm and a tart smile.

"I don't need him to propose. I just need you to have some fun," Becky retorted. "Last time you came to see me in San Antonio, I had to practically arm wrestle you to get there. You don't return calls. You stopped going to church. You're shutting everyone out. Maybe it's the grief, or maybe you just don't want any of us around anymore."

Hurt and humiliated by her friend's blunt words, Jennifer took a deep breath. "I'm sorry but I've been trying to get everything back in order here—and now this vandalism thing is in the way. Once I get this place renovated and have some breathing room, I'll get back into the swing of things."

"And what if that never happens?" Becky asked, a hand on Jennifer's arm. "What if you can't make it work?"

"I will, somehow. Don't tell me you've given up on me, too, Becky."

Becky put a hand around her shoulder. "I haven't given up on you, no, ma'am. But I do worry that you're in over your head here. What if you run out of money? What then?"

"I'm on a strict budget. I hope to bring in money when things get back on track. I have to."

"Your father wouldn't want you to work yourself to death on this place. You could easily go to work at the zoo in Austin. Didn't they offer you a job?"

Tempering her anger, Jennifer pulled away. "I don't want to work at the Austin Zoo, Bec. I want to work here. And I'm sorry you think I've been neglecting you."

"It's not me I'm worried about," Becky replied. "It's you. I mean, the only reason I was able to see you tonight is because you needed someone here with you while that security man looks around."

Jennifer whirled to stare at her friend. "You think I'm using you?"

"Of course not. I was thrilled to be invited. But you seem to have a hard time asking for help. Or just asking a friend to come and keep you company."

Jennifer couldn't deny that. "It has been a while since we've all had a girls' night out. I'll try to do better when this is over, I promise."

"Do it for yourself," Becky said. She reached out and hugged Jennifer close. "It's late. Let's go to bed. Things will look better—"

She stopped, stepping back to gasp, her finger pointing toward the window. "Jennifer, look."

Jennifer pivoted around. "What?" Then she saw it. "Is that fire?"

Bright golden flames flared into the night. And they were coming from the barn and stables.

Jennifer started running toward the door, adrenaline and fear catching in her throat. "Becky, call 911. The barn is on fire."

NINE

Jennifer grabbed her cell phone, hitting buttons to bring up Anderson's number. Holding the phone to her ear, she ran toward the stables, the sound of frightened horses whinnying and thrashing sending her into a mad sprint.

"What is it?" Anderson said on the second ring.

"Fire. The stables and barn."

"I'll be there. Don't go in—"

Jennifer put her phone in her shirt pocket and kept running, her heart colliding with her ribs, her breath hitching as she gulped in acrid, smoke-filled air. The lonely fire station a few miles down the road was manned mostly by volunteers with a pump truck. How long would it take for the pumper and a ladder truck to get here?

Glancing back, she saw Becky running toward her. "They're on the way," Becky shouted. "I drove up and opened the gate."

"I have to get the horses out." Jennifer rushed forward, opening the doors just wide enough to squeeze through. The fire was taking over the back of the barn where she stored equipment and feed. If she hurried, she might be able to set the horses loose before the flames touched on the hay bales closer to the stalls.

"Don't go in there," Becky called, running toward the open doors. "Jennifer!"

"I have to."

Jennifer scoped the fire on the other end of the long aisle and the distance between it and the last horse stall near the equipment barn—Sadie was in that one. The little mare was whinnying and snorting in fear. Pushing the door open farther so the other two horses could get through, she hurried up the alley.

"I'm coming, Sadie," Jennifer called, grabbing a blanket from one of the stalls. Opening stalls as fast as she could, she breathed a sigh of relief as the first two horses rushed toward the slim opening at the doors and into the night.

Thank goodness Anderson had Chestnut. But Sadie was still in her stall and she could be shy and excitable at times. She might not want to leave. Big puffs of smoke rose, blinding Jennifer as the fire greedily tore through a stack of boxes and lapped at the upper rafters.

Jennifer finally reached the stall, her nerves tinged with fear and fatigue, when two strong arms pulled her back.

"Get out of here now," Anderson ordered, grabbing the blanket from her. "Go, Jennifer."

"But Sadie," Jennifer said, tears forming in her eyes. "She's afraid."

He put a hand over his mouth, the smell of burning hay and wood all around them. "I've got her. Go."

Jennifer backed out of the stables, wiping at the soot

on her face, tears streaming freely now. She turned at the doors, searching for Becky.

Her friend rushed to gather Jennifer into her arms. "I managed to corral one of the horses. The other one ran for the hills. But they're safe."

Jennifer nodded, holding on to Becky. "Anderson's trying to bring Sadie out." The sound of sirens screaming brought her head up. "I hope they hurry."

Then she heard a loud crash and turned to see a burning rafter on the other side of the barn shudder and crash to the floor, taking out a stall's gate with it. "Anderson?"

Jennifer moved toward the doors again but Becky held her back. "The fire department is here, Jennifer. Let them do their job."

Jennifer sobbed a breath then motioned to the men rushing by with pick axes and fire extinguishers. "My friend is in there with one of my horses."

Two firemen took off into the barn while the rest of the crew worked to set up their equipment. Jennifer noticed the local sheriff car coming up the lane, too.

"Where is he?" she cried out. "I shouldn't have let him go in there."

"*You* went in there," Becky reminded her, clutching her close in the chilly night air.

Jennifer closed her eyes and lifted her head. "Please, Lord, let him be safe. Don't let anything happen to Anderson."

All she could do now was stand here and wait, her thoughts swirling in confusion just like the embers reaching up toward the stars. What if Anderson didn't make it? How could she live with that?

Then she looked up to see him emerging through the big doors, tugging Sadie with a lasso. He'd covered her head with a night rug but he yanked it off once they were clear, then he let the frightened horse go free.

Jennifer fell to her knees as she watched Sadie galloping by. Sadie went straight to where Chestnut stood, agitated and tethered, by a fence with the one Becky had corralled. The horses whinnied and stomped, their dark eyes wide with apprehension.

She turned to find Anderson kneeling to help her up. Jennifer looked him over, and, her knees trembling, rushed into his arms. "Thank you. Thank you so much." After hugging him tight, she stood back and fisted his arm. "But you shouldn't have done that. You could have been hurt."

"*I* shouldn't have done that?" Anger and adrenaline made his voice rise. His eyes looked golden in the firelight. "*You* were in there. You went in after I tried to tell you not to. What else was I supposed to do?"

Seeing the anger in his eyes, Jennifer stumbled back, her hands clutching the belt of her plush robe. "I'm sorry. I had to save my animals."

"At what cost, Jennifer? When will you realize this thing is dangerous—especially to you? Next time, they'll set your house on fire, with you in it."

Hurt by his harsh words, she looked down at her soiled slippers. "I know how dangerous things are around here, Anderson. But I don't know how to react, other than by taking action to protect what's mine." With a shrug and a twist toward Becky, she said, "Thanks again for saving Sadie. I'm going to see if my barn and stables can be saved."

A strong arm slipped around her wrist and brought her back. "I'm sorry," he said, his gaze as full of fire as the barn behind him. "I didn't see you when I rode up. And when Becky told me you were in there…I had to do something."

"And you did," she replied, her tone going soft and breathless. "And so did I when I realized it was on fire. I'm okay and Sadie is safe, thanks to you. I owe you a lot."

He tugged her close. "And maybe that's what's really bothering you. Maybe you don't want to owe me."

"Maybe so," she said, lifting away as the fire chief and the sheriff came toward her. "I need to see how bad the damage is."

Anderson let her go, but his eyes held hers for a long minute before he stomped away and pulled out his phone.

"Setting the barn on fire. Not very original but very effective," Anderson said, spitting the words into the phone. "They're escalating things, Ben. And I have to wonder if my presence here is the reason."

"What makes you think that?"

Anderson watched as firemen wearing heavy turnout equipment came and went, busy carrying fire rakes and ladders to salvage what was left of the big barn. "She hadn't had anything this bad happen until I showed up."

"Have you considered that she might not have noticed anything happening until you did show up, not to mention we have one of their men in custody and we took him in right before you were assigned to monitor that site? They would have tried to get to her sooner or later and they've probably been watching her all along. Now they must think good old Eddie Jimenez spilled more than he actually did. You yourself said things would probably get worse. So now they have."

Anderson looked over to where Jennifer huddled with Becky near the traumatized horses. At least the other animals—the cows and goats and that infernal llama—were out in the pasture. "For some reason they're not moving on to a new drop site. And that means there must be something around here they don't want us to find." He told Ben his theory regarding the inactive security lights and cameras.

"Now that makes sense," Ben replied. "How bad is the barn?"

Anderson looked past the two women. "The back half is gone and the rest is charred. I just hope she's got good insurance. The sheriff's here, too. I'll have to talk to him."

"Talk to the fire inspector or the chief, find out if they can determine the point of origin and any signs of arson."

"That shouldn't be hard," Anderson replied. "Somebody walked right in the place and torched it."

"Let the fire department do its job while you go over things with the sheriff. He knows Jennifer was attacked, too. I can send Cade or Oliver to help you sweep the place first thing tomorrow so we can file a report," Ben replied. "And Anderson, remind Miss Rodgers that she might have to consider staying somewhere else for a while."

"She won't do that with all these animals to care for,

I can assure you," Anderson said on a testy note. "The woman almost got herself in a heap of trouble tonight, trying to save one of her horses."

"Do what you can to find out what's so important that they'd set fire to the place. For all we know they could have drugs hidden all over her property. If they think she's been monitoring their comings and goings with security cameras, they'll keep targeting her."

Anderson hung up, the edginess he'd felt all night doubled now. Something didn't seem right. Why set a fire in the barn if they were after something they'd hidden?

Then the fire chief walked up, shaking his head. "Looks like somebody threw a gasoline-soaked bag full of old rags right inside the back doors. The rags didn't burn up, but the straw around them sure caught up. The entire structure is unsound now. She'll need to tear it down and rebuild the whole thing."

Anderson took in the grim news. "Can I have a look now?"

"Yeah, but be careful. We're checking for hot spots to make sure it's out but for now, it looks to be contained."

Anderson gave the waiting sheriff a quick explanation with a promise to call him first thing in the morning, then walked over to Jennifer. "Guess you heard?"

She nodded, her arms wrapped around her body, her gaze slamming into his. "My barn is gone. These people need to leave me alone."

"Yeah, they do. But they won't." He took off his jacket and put it around her shoulders. "I've got to look things over. Why don't you let Becky take you back to the house?"

She shook her head. "I have to take care of the horses. I'll put them in the shed out in the corral for tonight."

"I'll help," Becky said. "I'll run and get us both a warm jacket and some gloves, okay?"

Jennifer nodded again. "Thanks." Then she turned back to Anderson. "At least it's not too cold tonight."

"No, the wind died down around sunset, thankfully. Or that fire could have been a lot worse."

She stared at the soggy, charred remains of her barn. "I guess I'll have to beg for help with this, too."

Anderson hated the defeat in her voice. "Do you have insurance?"

"Yes, but I'm sure my premiums will go up now." Pushing at her hair, she looked down at the ground. "Is there any way to get a message to these people? Tell them I don't know anything and I don't have anything?"

"Not a good idea. That would only confirm that you know about *them*."

"So I just have to live like this? Wondering what will happen next?"

"No, you don't." He put his hands on her arms. "I'm working real hard to figure this out, Jennifer. I need you to stay patient and not do anything foolish."

She stared up at him, her eyes as dark as the night. "The only thing I plan on doing is protecting my property, Anderson."

Anderson didn't like the challenge in her eyes. Or the force in her words. "Look, I'm going to go over every inch of this place until I find something, okay?

Tomorrow, I'll get the extra security measures in place and I'll talk to some of your nearest neighbors, including Mr. Chason." He'd haul the neighbor in for questioning in a more formal setting if need be if he located the man.

She put a hand to her head. "The construction crew is coming back tomorrow to finish the new pen. I can't postpone that. They're on a timeline and so am I."

"Let them get the work done. We don't have time to do checks on all of them so I'll be nearby and watching, once I get through questioning Mr. Chason. You'll have Becky here. And Jacob in the afternoon."

"I'm going to carry a pistol, just in case."

"Don't go anywhere by yourself, you hear?"

"I hear."

Her friend came back with the jackets and handed one to her. Jennifer lifted Anderson's coat off her shoulders and handed it back to him. "Go. We've got to get the animals settled."

Anderson took off with the sheriff toward the barn, sidestepping burned-out beams and mud spots, the smell of wet, charred wood and scorched hay assaulting him. He walked past the barn and took out his flashlight to search for tracks leading into the fence line and woods. It didn't take him long to find another tear in the chain-link fence not far from the big barn.

He'd managed to pry the earlier cut back together. Someone had cut the fence again. He held the flashlight down, finding footprint indentations in the grass and hard dirt. He followed the footprints up to the back of the barn where the mud and water from the fire hose had dissolved them.

Someone had come on to the property again, no doubt about that. He might be able to set a cast and get a shoe print, but finding the person wearing the shoe was another thing.

Maybe he should have staked out the barn instead of the new alligator pen.

Then he had a flash of clarity.

What if the fire had been a diversion?

A diversion to get him back to the house.

And away from that new pen and the cartel's drop site.

Stomping back toward the front of the barn, Anderson looked around and saw that Chestnut was still where he'd left him. Jennifer and Becky were busy inside the corral with the other horses. Not bothering to explain, Anderson tugged at Chestnut's reins and swung up on the big horse. Then he took off toward the unfinished gator pen.

But he had a bad feeling he wasn't going to like what he might find back there.

TEN

"Here, drink this." Becky forced Jennifer to take the hot tea. "And sit down before you collapse."

Jennifer numbly slid into the kitchen chair, her hands gripping the warmth of the big cup. "What time is it?"

"Almost six. The sun's rising."

Jennifer got up. "I have to call the insurance company and I have the morning feedings."

"Wait, Jen," Becky said, holding a hand up in the air. "First, rest and eat something. Then you can call the insurance people. And I've already called several volunteers and patrons to come and help with the feedings and the chores. That way you'll be free to worry about the barn and make sure the horses find temporary shelter."

Jennifer looked up at her friend, too grateful to speak at first. "Thank you. I'm so glad you're here."

Becky smiled, then took a sip of her own tea. "God has a way of putting people in the right place at the right time. Good thing Anderson was here, too."

While her friend went about slicing cinnamon bread for toast, Jennifer thought about Anderson. Had God sent him here at exactly the right time? And where was he right now?

Worried about him, she closed her eyes and remembered his harsh words to her last night. And the emotions beneath that harsh facade. She'd gone against his orders to stay out of the burning barn, so she could understand his anger. But she'd also seen something else there in his eyes. A fierce longing had shattered through his anger, a longing that mirrored what Jennifer had felt when *he'd* gone into that barn for *her* sake.

I can't think about that, she reasoned. *Once this is all over, he'll be out of my life.* Anderson would go back to his work and she'd return to her daily routine. Funny how her work and her scheduled tasks used to bring her such joy and satisfaction. But now…well, now she had Anderson underfoot and inside her head and he'd changed her whole perspective. She resented that even while she treasured his presence. Best not to depend on that presence, however.

"We have toast," Becky said, placing two crisp, buttered slices in front of Jennifer. "Don't let it get cold."

Jennifer took a bite, the sweet cinnamon mixed with crisp buttered bread sticking in her throat. She wasn't hungry, but she forced down a few more bites. "I'm in serious trouble, Becky."

"I know, honey," her friend said. "You've got double trouble from what I can see."

"What do you mean?"

Becky dropped her own toast and brushed crumbs off her fingers. "Your barn burned down and…you got one fine-looking man burning for your attention."

Shocked, Jennifer sat up and stared at her friend. Was it that obvious? "What are you talking about?"

Becky shook her head. "You always did have a one-track mind. In case you haven't noticed, that man is also in serious trouble."

"Yeah, he's trying to track down whoever is behind all of this, so that kind of puts a target on his back."

"Jen, quit trying to deny this," Becky said. "Anderson Michaels has two things on his mind right now. Get the bad guys and…get the girl. And I sure wish I could stick around to see which one he gets to first."

Exhaustion pulled at Anderson. Guiding Chestnut toward the corral shed, he dismounted and took care of the valiant gelding by quickly brushing him down and throwing a day rug over the big horse. "C'mon, boy. Let's find you some water and a bit of gruel to munch on."

After getting Chestnut housed in the open corral shed next to the other horses, Anderson stopped to have another look at the gutted remains of the barn, then slowly made his way up to the cabin. Cade was on his way to help Anderson go over everything again. A new set of eyes sure would help, but Anderson's suspicions about the barn fire being a distraction had been right on the money. Somebody had wanted him away from the back forty.

And someone had been messing around in the dirt near the chain-linked fence around the pond. What was back there? Drugs? Money? Or something else entirely?

He could speculate for days and get nowhere. Right

now, he wanted a good cup of coffee and a hot shower. So he headed straight to the bunkhouse, where he'd told Cade to meet him.

Okay, so maybe he was avoiding Jennifer, too, he thought as he got cleaned up and dressed. He still shook with anger each time he thought about her going into that barn, but in his heart he could understand the woman's love for her animals. He'd have done the same if his horse had been in danger. Still, his heart roared up and took off when he remembered their argument last night. And the way she'd looked when he'd chastised her.

I came down too hard, just like I always do, Anderson thought now as he entered the efficiency kitchen. His mother often reminded him that he let his temper get the best of his better judgment, just like his daddy. But a man tended to do that when he cared too much.

That realization floored him and alerted him. He needed to reel in his feelings for Jennifer so he could take care of business. Stay on course, get this case going and…move on? He'd always been able to do that before.

But he knew when this was over, he wouldn't be able to move on. Jennifer had taken hold of him in the worst kind of way. And how was he supposed to handle that when he was caught in the middle of one of the biggest cases he'd ever worked?

"Lord, I could use some guidance here," Anderson said out loud while the coffee perked and gulped. With each beat of the drip, drip from the percolator, Anderson said a prayer. "Teach me, help me, show me what is right, Lord."

Anderson closed his eyes to the fatigue and asked God to give him some peace. First, the case. Then he'd figure out what to do about his feelings for Jennifer.

Of course, he had to find out if she even cared about his feelings to begin with, after last night.

Becky nudged Jennifer after they'd gone down to the barn to look at the mess. "Mercy, girl, now there's two of them."

Jennifer glanced toward the bunkhouse and saw Anderson out on the porch talking to a beefy-looking man with thick dark blond hair. "Now who is that?"

"Let's go find out," Becky suggested with a grin.

Jennifer pulled her friend along. "Whatever they're discussing probably involves me, so yes, let's go and listen in." She looked back at the barn. "I can't do anything down there until the insurance agent shows up, anyway. And thanks to you, all the other chores are being handled."

"I'm that kind of friend," Becky retorted with a wink.

Anderson glanced up when he saw them coming. "Morning."

Could he be any more evasive? Jennifer thought even while she managed to avoid making eye contact with him.

"Hello." She decided to look at his friend instead. "What's up?"

"Jennifer, this is Cade Jarvis. I brought him in to help me search for evidence and go over things at the barn and the new alligator pen again."

Cade reached out a hand and gave Jennifer a hearty handshake. "Hello, ma'am. Sorry about all of this."

Jennifer accepted his handshake. "Thank you. This is my friend, Becky." At Anderson's questioning look, she added, "I told her what's going on."

After more handshakes and small talk, Jennifer asked, "So I assume you're here to help figure this out, since Anderson called you."

"Yes, ma'am."

"Stop with the ma'am thing."

"Yes. Okay."

Anderson shifted on his boots. "While the barn was on fire, someone went snooping near the new pen."

"What?" Jennifer put her hands on her hips then stared out toward the trees. "This happened last night?"

"Yep. A distraction to get me away from that area," Anderson replied, still looking anywhere but at her.

Becky didn't seem to have any problems looking at Anderson. "So what do you two plan to do about that?"

Cade cleared his throat. "All we can do at this point is keep watching and try to figure out what these people want. I believe they think your security cameras have them on tape. They want any evidence you might have."

Becky lifted her head, her eyes on Jennifer. "Jen, this is about more than just security, right?"

Jennifer finally looked over at Anderson. What could she say?

Anderson saw her confusion. "You know we're Texas Rangers. We think the cartel is targeting this place because they've been messing in drugs. And I'm only telling you this for your protection and because I might need you to help Jennifer out again before this is over."

Becky hissed a breath. "Of course. Need me to sit in on a stakeout?"

"No, not that kind of help," Anderson replied. "This is dangerous. You need to stay close to Jennifer and stay away from back there. And this conversation can't be repeated. Got it?"

"Got it," Becky said, her gaze lifting over to Jennifer. "This is worse than I thought."

"A lot worse," Jennifer replied. "And I've got the construction crew arriving any minute now."

"Just go about your business," Anderson said. "We're heading back there right now—before they stir things up even more."

"You'd better hurry," Jennifer said, still cranky for lack of sleep and too much stress. "I called the foreman and they'll be here by nine."

Anderson looked at his watch. "That gives us a good hour. We'll head out there first, then come back to inspect the barn again." He shot Cade a glance. "I need to talk to Jennifer in private."

Cade took the hint. "I'll drive on out and get started. You can meet me there later." He tipped his hat at the women and got in his truck.

Becky stood there, still watching Cade. "Is he single?"

"Yes," Anderson said. "But highly devoted to his job."

Just like you, Jennifer wanted to shout out. His words were an obvious hint to her, no doubt.

Becky looked back at them. "Oh, okay. Got it. And you want me gone, right?"

"Do you mind?" Jennifer asked, giving Anderson a glaring look. "You can check on Boudreaux and Bobby Wayne and make sure they've had their morning meal. Be careful and stay outside the first fence."

"I know how to handle your alligators," Becky said over her shoulder. "They're about the only two of the male species I think I can understand."

She pranced off, leaving an uncomfortable silence in her wake.

"Your friend's spunky."

"I like that about her."

Jennifer didn't know what else to say. Then Anderson took her hand in his and looked her square in the eyes. "Jennifer, I'm sorry about how I acted last night. I get so caught up in my cases, sometimes I take my frustrations out on other people. I sure didn't mean to do that with you."

She wanted to stay mad at him but the way his eyes had turned all golden and shimmering made her mouth water and her heart skip a few beats. "Last night was difficult for all of us."

His hand moved up her arm. "But…I should remember that you didn't ask for this and…I kind of stormed in here, telling you what I needed to do, never thinking how traumatic this would be for you."

Why was he being so nice now, when she felt so bad about every little thing?

"It's okay. I'm stronger than I look."

"I can believe that." He moved close, so close she saw the flecks of rich brown in his eyes. When he reached up to push a few wisps of hair off her temple, Jennifer knew she was in too deep. "I don't want to hurt you. I'd never want to do that."

She allowed the one delicate shiver to chase down her spine. "Is that an apology or a warning?"

"I am sorry," he said. "But…I am warning you—I have to keep my mind on my job. The stakes are too high, otherwise."

She pulled away, hurt by his bluntness. "Like I didn't see that from the get-go. No time for anything else, right?"

He hit a hand against his jeans, his face covered with frustration. "I'm doing this all wrong. I've never been good with words. Never been good with women, truth be told. But…with you…it's hard to explain."

"You don't need to explain anything," she retorted, her heart tearing. "You're telling me that you don't want any more distractions—especially from me, right?"

"It's not like that. I like…being distracted by you but—"

"But any distraction is a risk, and you don't want to take a risk with me. Well, guess what, cowboy, I don't want to risk anything with you, either. Just do what you've got to do, Anderson, and then let me get on with my work and my life. Because I learned firsthand that men like you—men who live for their careers—don't stick around for any kind of distractions that might actually require a commitment."

With that, she turned and stomped away before she made a fool of herself and asked him why he couldn't make an exception for her and break all his tightly held rules.

Just once, she'd like to know what it felt like to be loved, truly loved, instead of being left abandoned and longing for something she'd never have.

ELEVEN

Cade stared down at the freshly turned dirt just outside the chain-link fence then took a picture. "We could do some digging ourselves, maybe find something."

"We could," Anderson replied, the cold, cloudy morning not helping his black mood. "Or we could wait 'em out. If they want this bad enough, they'll be back. And I'd rather catch 'em in the act than make a mess digging up things right now. If we let them do the work, it should save us a lot of problems with Jennifer Rodgers."

"Good point." Cade took another picture. "You didn't see anything last night?"

"No. They made sure I'd go running back to the main house, which means they've seen me back here and they know something's up. But they didn't get very far from the looks of these shallow shovel holes."

"Might be watching right now," Cade said on a low even tone. "Maybe they were just planning on messing things up to force a shutdown, stall for time."

"Probably." Anderson ventured a glance around the woods. "They won't come out again until dark. Cowards tend to do that. But they're getting bolder." He put his hands on his hips. "Any word on the Lions?"

"Nothing much other than what we already know. We just need one name but Jimenez sure is afraid to give up the goods."

"And still nothing on our coma patient, either," Anderson said, huffing a breath. "I'm getting mighty antsy."

"Does that have anything to do with that pretty dark-headed woman you kept staring at earlier?"

Anderson kicked at the dirt, his gaze scanning the area once again in case he'd missed anything. "They had to have come in on foot. I don't see horse tracks or car tracks. And with all the mud and packed dirt, it's hard to find any firm shoe imprints." He stomped at the mud. "We need to hurry this up and go over the barn again. Too many people milling around."

Cade held the camera toward the fence line and clicked. "I take it your non-answer means Jennifer is getting to you in a big way."

"I'm trying to focus on the problem at hand," Anderson shot back. "She's all caught up in this case."

"That's what I'm saying," Cade replied. "Is *she* a problem?"

Anderson pushed at his hat. "She might be. I'm not sure yet. She resents me being here right now. We've had words a few times." He couldn't tell his friend things between Jennifer and him were on a highly emotional level right now. It wasn't cool to get so involved with a subject in an active case.

Cade gave him a look full of questions. "I see."

"I gotta go talk to that missing neighbor and work on making the security around here better," Anderson said. "Why don't we head back to the stables and see if the insurance inspector is here yet."

"No problem," Cade replied, following him. "Anything from this site I need to take back to headquarters?"

"No. I've sent in everything as far as evidence, but we don't have a leg to stand on right now. I just need to find out about the background checks on a couple of people." He pulled out his phone and called Ben about that. But he didn't miss the inquisitive expression on Cade's face.

"The kid's clean," Ben said. "Nothing there. But that neighbor, Chason, has a list of complaints against him regarding property lines and privacy issues. He's been before city councils and planning boards in just about every place he's lived. And, get this—he's had some misdemeanors regarding possession of pot. He's one of those naturalists who believes marijuana should be legal. A live wire and a possible person of interest behind these latest incidents, especially the joint y'all found out there. We can't rule him out."

"I'm on my way to find him," Anderson said on a snarl.

"Thanks." He filled Cade in on what Ben had told him.

Cade gave him a sideways stare, then turned toward his truck. "While you talk to Chason, I'll go over the fire scene. A fresh pair of eyes might spot something you didn't see."

Anderson nodded. "You might be right on that. Thanks for riding out. I'll check back with you in about an hour or so."

He got in his own truck and followed Cade back up the winding lane, everything he needed to do today front and center in his mind. If he could get past the woman who was also front and center in his mind.

A day later, things were hopping around the farm, Jennifer thought as she took a long drink of water around midday. On a normal weekday morning, she would have enjoyed the buzz of activity all around her. But today, she had the gaping hole in the back of the charred barn to remind her why the insurance inspector was here and she had extra volunteers to remind her that she'd had yet another setback and couldn't keep up by herself. She had the construction crews and landscaping trucks driving back and forth along the lane toward the alligator pond to remind her that at least she'd be able to move the two alligators to a better habitat, possibly tomorrow or next week.

And she had Anderson to remind her of the danger lurking around every corner, causing her to lose trust in herself and to wonder if this whole operation would ever become a reality. With all the commotion, she just prayed no one would slip up and blurt out the awful truth to her board members and donors. Right now, the story stood at vandalism and that was, right now, the truth. She didn't have any proof to who was actually doing this. And she had too much to do today to even try to figure it out or worry about it.

But Anderson seemed to be on the case even if he was in such a foul mood he practically scared all the volunteers almost as much as old Boudreaux did. After

he'd returned from Mr. Chason's, he'd installed better
door locks and dead bolts. And he and Cade had set
up some sort of easy-to-install, invisible fence monitor
around the perimeter of the alligator pen, explaining to
anyone curious enough to notice that Jennifer was tired
of the vandalism and needed to protect herself and her
animals, and the vandals, too, at that. It wasn't on right
now, since too many people were coming and going.
But it would be on tonight. And Anderson would be
out there waiting and watching. Jennifer would have a
monitor on inside the house, too.

No one seemed to care about the tall, cranky Ranger
working at a frenzied pace with security, however. The
construction crew had been grilled and questioned even
while they grudgingly helped with tacking the invisible fence monitors on to the existing fences. She didn't
know if he'd found anything or anyone suspicious with
that group. Anderson didn't seem very forthcoming with
the details.

And he'd come back from the Chason ranch to inform
her that Ralph Chason was not on the property. Anderson did tell her on a low growl that he'd done a thorough
search but hadn't found a vehicle on the premises, either.
Now she was beginning to worry that something bad
had happened to her persnickety old neighbor. What if
he'd stumbled upon the drug runners and been hurt or
worse?

When she saw Anderson coming around the corner
of the goat pen late in the day, she headed toward him,
determined to make him talk. "I'm worried about Mr.
Chason."

Anderson stopped, his frown still intact. Would he ever get over their harsh words from last night? Would she?

"Maybe he works in the city or something, I don't know. But our check indicated he worked at home. I peeked into his art studio and everything seemed in order. I called out his name and identified myself several times. I don't think he was hiding. And his garage was empty, too. He could be on a trip."

"He does go out scouting all over the state for wood and rocks a lot," Jennifer replied. "That could be it." Relaxing a little, she offered Anderson a fresh bottle of water. "I have to go see about the progress on the pen."

At least that got his attention. "You don't need to be back there alone."

"I won't be alone. The whole work crew is back there along with several reliable volunteers."

He frowned but didn't argue. "We went over the barn again and didn't find anything beyond the gasoline-soaked rags and since the insurance adjuster and the fire captain ruled it an arson, you can clean up now. Jacob is down there with a whole crew, moving beams and breaking down the damaged walls."

"I'll have to rebuild the whole thing," she said.

"Yes, and I'm sorry about that. Somebody meant business. They're escalating the threats just like I expected, and I'm convinced it's because they think you've recorded their activities. I'd better go help Jacob. Maybe I'll spot something."

He gave her one last blank look, then turned to leave.

She almost let him go, but something tugged at her. "Anderson?"

He turned, the dark clouds behind him reminding her that rain might move in before nightfall. "Yeah?"

"Can we be friends again? I mean, I know I didn't take this very seriously at first, but...I was scared last night. I didn't think. I just ran into the barn. It was a mistake, but...I wish you wouldn't hold it against me."

She saw the torment in his burnished eyes. "I don't hold it against you," he said as he stalked back toward her. "And I'm sorry if I've been rude today. I've just got a lot on my mind." His look indicated she was part of that.

"Me, too. This thing has forced us together and I guess we're taking it out on each other, huh?"

He almost smiled then. "Yeah, I reckon. I get frustrated when a criminal gets the best of me. And I should have seen that coming last night. Setting the barn on fire is a time-honored coward's way of scaring people."

"You had no way of knowing they did it as a diversion."

"No, I didn't. But then, I was more worried about getting you to safety than turning and heading back to catch them in the act."

His blunt nature stung her, but the gentle look in his eyes tempered her and held her. "Can we work together from now on? You seem to be condemning me and blaming me."

He rushed toward her then, his hands pulling at her arms. "No, no, you've got it all wrong there, Jennifer. I don't blame you. I...how can I explain it? I can't get past how I felt when I thought you might die inside that fire.

All I could think was what a shame that would be—the world without you here in it—you taking care of these animals, showing children how to do the same, protecting creatures that can't always protect themselves." He stopped, looked around and leaned close. "I thought about how kissing you made me feel and my heart just about burned up faster than that barn. I don't know what's happening."

She touched a hand to his chest, her smile small and reluctant. "You thought all of that…last night?"

His lips tilted. "Okay, I thought about the kiss right away and then I didn't think beyond that until I had you out of that barn." With what seemed an embarrassed shrug, he shook his head. "And then when Sadie didn't want to come out, I thought about all the rest, to keep myself calm, to keep myself alive so I could…maybe tell you all of that. And keep that stubborn, scared horse alive, too."

Jennifer stood looking up at him, her mind whirling with images of rafters falling and horses bolting. That's how he made her feel—as if the barn were on fire and she was helpless to put out the flames. Not knowing what to say, and not understanding where this might lead since he'd indicated he was all about the case and not her, she smiled up at him. "I'm sure glad you kept that horse alive, Anderson."

That made his eyes crinkle and his lips twist.

He stepped back, fighting a grin. "Me, too. I'll be back later so we can talk."

"Okay."

She watched him go, so glad that she'd had the nerve to confront him. Anderson didn't seem to be a man of words. He had a quiet strength that didn't demand attention. But that kind of strength could sure fill a room.

And a woman's heart.

TWELVE

Today was the day.

Jennifer slipped on her oldest pair of wading boots and grabbed an apple. It was time to move Boudreaux and Bobby Wayne to their fancy new home. She prayed there wouldn't be any more trouble.

She chewed on the sweet, red apple, trying to put images of fire and shadowy figures out of her mind. The last couple of days since the barn fire had been thankfully quiet around here. Becky was back and taking care of the birds in the aviary today and she had helpers lined up to feed the corralled animals so Jennifer could take care of the gators.

Since Anderson had been staking out the new pen, the vandalism had stopped. But she only had to look at the tense lines in his face to see that this wasn't over yet. It would be a while before she could rebuild the barn but in the meantime, it had been cleaned and sealed off. She was thankful the insurance should cover most of the renovations.

The vet had checked over the horses and other animals and declared all of them fit. Another blessing. And she had a team of volunteers on loan from the San

Antonio Zoo coming in to help contain and transport the alligators.

Now if she could just assure Anderson that moving the alligators as soon as possible was the right thing to do.

He didn't like the idea. He'd told her so last night. "It's too dangerous right now, Jennifer. A lot could go wrong."

But she'd put her foot down. "Anderson, I can't hold off. I've had people on standby for months now. Everyone's arranged their schedules and it's now or never. Drug runners or no drug runners."

And that would explain why he stood off to the side, sulking like an ever-watchful big cat, while everyone around him talked in excited tones. Anderson obviously liked to be in control of a situation, but moving two gigantic reptiles wasn't in his playbook. He didn't think the gators should be moved until his investigation was finished, but Jennifer couldn't wait for that. With few leads and no solid evidence of what was going on, they were in limbo. She could deal with it, but she wouldn't make her animals suffer or wait.

And her alligators had been waiting months for a better habitat. So today was the day and Ranger-man would just have to live with that.

Jennifer didn't waste any time making a beeline right to the intimidating Ranger. He had a serious avoidance issue. The man didn't like to talk things out, unless it had to do with his aggravating case, of course.

"How are you?" she asked, her smile bright and full of a courage she didn't feel.

"I'm just fine," he said, tipping a finger in the air like a salute.

Yeah, Jennifer could see the "fine" all over him. Even dressed in khaki pants and an old work shirt, the man cut a striking pose. Several of her female helpers had sighed each time they walked past Anderson.

"Want to watch the process?" she asked, hoping she could show him that she actually knew what she was doing.

"I don't know if I can watch," he said, his expression bordering on apprehensive. "I mean, they're both kind of big. And they have big teeth. What if you get your arm bitten off?"

"We know how to deal with that," Jennifer replied, thinking he looked really cute when he was just a tad afraid. His concern for her softened her feelings for him even more and caused some of her own anxiety to level off. "Just stand out of the way, Ranger-man."

"I'm not scared for myself," he said on a defensive tone. "But…I'm wondering how someone as tiny as you…and wearing bright blue waders embossed with yellow rubber ducks…could possibly wrestle something that powerful."

"Watch and learn," she said, striding away. He'd noticed her waders. That was kind of sweet.

Putting thoughts of Anderson and his endearing, confusing ways out of her mind, Jennifer rallied the team. "Okay, y'all know the drill. We contain them, tape their snouts and secure their legs, then we lift them with the crane and drop them inside the crates." She pointed to the two long plywood crates they'd use to transport the alligators on the back of a pickup truck. "Once the boys are inside the crates, we'll let Dr. Jenkins examine them to make sure they're up to this and then we're off to the new pond." *And please, Lord, don't let me find anything crazy or illegal going on back there.* Lifting her head, she called out to the zoo biologist. "Okay, get ready to feed the bait line. Let's get this done."

Then she gathered her hooks and the lasso she'd use to catch the alligators and headed into the shallow water.

Anderson's heart raced like a herd of wild ponies. He didn't think he could stand out of the way, even if Jennifer had suggested that very thing. How could he let her march right in there with those brutes, and wearing the cutest pair of duck-covered waders at that? It was almost as bad as having to watch her take the alligators to a spot that by all rights should be cordoned off as a possible crime scene.

Reminding himself that Jennifer knew her stuff and that she was excited about getting this under way, Anderson bit back the need to offer her advice and counsel and decided he'd have to think long and hard about falling for a woman who knew no fear. Because she scared him all the way down to his boots.

Jennifer went into warrior mode, circling back behind where the gators had pulled up in the shallows to enjoy some bad-smelling raw meat. Taking slow, measured steps, she went after unpredictable Bobby Wayne first, sneaking up on the big alligator's backside and with the help of some nearby strong-armed nuisance trappers, lassoing the gator before he could finish his meaty appetizer.

Anderson let out a breath and then watched as Jennifer straddled the gator and quickly wrapped his jaws shut with strong duct tape. Even though she'd explained that this was safe if you knew what you were doing, Anderson prayed she was right.

Closing his eyes in a vivid prayer, he held to the fence so he wouldn't rush forward and drag her away from that tail-wagging alligator. But he needn't have worried. The trappers helped Jennifer with the tape, then quickly secured his legs as if he were a wanted criminal being handcuffed. After using the crane to help lift the now-still alligator into his crate, they cajoled Boudreaux, who'd retreated to the deep side of the pond, back to get his treat then lassoed him into a flip. On his back now, his underbelly glistening in the early morning sun, the old gator seemed to go into a quiet trance.

Maybe like Anderson, the gator was having a heart attack.

"Let's flip him," Jennifer called. "It's okay, Boudreaux. Just going for a nice little ride."

And then with the help of the trappers on either side, she flipped the big snarling gator over again, careful to get out of the way of his swatting-mad tail. Soon, poor Boudreaux was taped and handcuffed and ready to be read his rights. He went into a crate beside Bobby Wayne and both alligators had a thorough exam from Dr. Jenkins.

"Fit and fancy," the gray-haired vet declared.

The zoologists examined the alligators to their satisfaction, too. And then the boys were quickly freed of their taped snouts and legs and the crates were shut up tight.

Everyone clapped in relief. And Anderson let out a sigh, beads of sweat cooling his backbone. His job now was to watch for any human varmints at the site.

Jennifer turned toward Anderson, a big smile radiating across her face. "Time to upgrade your habitat," she said as she patted Boudreaux's big box. "Let's go," she called to her many helpers.

Then she waved to him. "Coming?"

"Yes, ma'am," he called, his breath still coming way too quick. He liked Jennifer's looks and her spunk already. But now, his feelings of awe and amazement had taken on new heights.

The woman had just wrestled two alligators.

And what wasn't there to love about a woman who could do that while wearing rubber ducky boots? He wondered as he got in his truck and followed the convoy down to the new pen.

Halfway toward the pen, Anderson got a call from Ben.

"We finally got a hit on the photos we put out on the coma patient. You know that neighbor you've been looking for, Chason? He called in this morning and said he thinks he's seen the man in the photo."

Anderson stopped his truck, letting it idle while he jotted notes. "You don't say? I went to Chason's place several times and he either wasn't at home or he was hiding."

"He claims he was in Dallas on business. Just got back late yesterday and saw the photo on the news," Ben replied. "Go back over to his place and see what he says. Could just be a ploy to protest the alligator compound."

"I'll get right on it," Anderson said. He did a U-turn on the grass and headed away from the alligator pond and right on out the open gates of the rescue compound. He'd catch up with Jennifer later. Right now, she was in a controlled crowd, so she should be safe until he got back.

A few minutes later, Anderson once again stood at the door of Ralph Chason's barn-like studio. No point in pretending with this man about why he was here. Chason would have to know Anderson was here in an official capacity. "Mr. Chason, I need a word with you, sir."

The door swung open and a man with long gray bushy hair stood there wearing a chambray shirt and old worn jeans.

Anderson flashed his badge. "Ranger Anderson Michaels. Can I come in?"

"Do I have a choice in the matter?" Chason shot back. But he waved Anderson inside the cluttered confines of his work space. "I told that fellow I talked to on the phone I can't be too sure about this."

Anderson had hoped for a more definite report. "Let's just talk about things and see."

Chason motioned to a rickety old chair next to a scarred desk. "Take a load off, son."

Anderson glanced around at the eccentric artwork lining the long building. "Can I ask where you've been the last couple of days, sir?"

"What business is that of yours?"

The man was obstinate, that was for sure. And Anderson's antennae immediately went up. All that bluster could be hiding something sinister. "Just getting my facts straight since I've been informed you have a beef with Miss Rodgers over her new alligator pond."

"That ain't got a bit to do with me running into that squatter back there," Chason replied.

"I think it does," Anderson said, dropping the conversational tone and going into intimidating law enforcement mode. "Especially if you had anything to do with the vandalism and fire on Miss Rodgers's property."

"What vandalism? And a fire? I been in Dallas setting up an exhibit at an art gallery, young man. So if you're here to accuse me of something, just spit it out so we can clear things up."

Deciding to change his tactics, Anderson pulled a copy of the coma patient's photo out of his pocket. "Is this the man you think you saw, sir?"

Chason put on his glasses and squinted at the photo. "Well, he didn't look this bad when I spotted him, but yeah, I'd say that's the man."

Anderson jotted that down. "And when and where exactly did you see him?"

Chason grunted. "A few months ago, back there on the property being overrun by Miss Rodgers."

"You mean the property she bought and is adding to her rescue compound?"

"Yeah, the very same," Chason said, his tone dismissive. "I tried to tell her to stay away from back there. I think something fishy is going on, but that woman is as stubborn as a mule. Didn't listen to me."

"You mean all your threats toward her were to warn

her off?" Anderson said, surprised at this new take on things.

Chason pushed at some drawings on his messy desk. "No. I didn't want anybody back there since it runs into my property and I like my privacy, but that spot seems to be mighty popular with vagrants. I was out there looking for materials to work with when I spotted a campsite and found your John Doe shouting into a cell phone. And he wasn't too happy with whoever he was shouting at, let me tell you."

"Do you remember the exact date?"

Chason named a day about six months back. That was a while before Gregory Pike had been murdered, the unidentified man lying in a coma found beside him.

"Did you hear what he said?" Anderson asked, waiting for Chason to respond.

"I heard enough," Chason replied. "Something about needing to take care of the matter before things got out of hand. I don't know what the other person said to him, but he went on to say he hadn't signed up for this kind of thing. He wanted his pay so he could split—or at least that's what it sounded like to me."

"Did you confront the man?"

"I sure did. Me and my shotgun, that is. Told him to get off the property. He glared at me but he left when he saw I meant business. That was before I knew the property had been sold to Jennifer Rodgers. I had thought about buying it up, but she beat me to the draw. And when I found out about her putting alligators back there and fencing the woods off, I got real mad."

"But not mad enough to ransack her tack room or set fire to her stables?"

"I told you, boy, I didn't do any of that. You're barking up the wrong tree there and you can verify my whereabouts by calling the gallery in Dallas. Probably that Irishman's friends paying her a visit, up to no good."

"Irishman? What do you mean?"

Chason looked up, his aged eyes squinting at Anderson. "The man I talked to and warned away—he had an Irish accent. Don't get that a lot around these parts."

"Are you sure?" Anderson asked, dumbfounded. What would an Irishman have to do with a Mexican drug cartel?

"Of course I'm sure," Chason shot back. "I heard the man. Before he saw that I was willing to shoot first and ask questions later, he told me I was trespassing on private property and told *me* to get gone. Only he was doing it with a heavy Irish brogue. I ducked behind some shrubs, but I had my twelve gauge trained on him, so I made him leave instead. But for the life of me, I can't figure why an Irishman would be camping out on a remote pasture in South Texas."

Anderson looked over at the old man staring up at him. He could imagine only one reason why the Irishman was back there. He must have been involved with the drug runners. Which fitted in somehow with him being shot at Gregory Pike's house. Why else would this man have been at Gregory's house that day?

But if the mysterious Irishman was with either the cartel or the Lions, why had one of his own shot him and put him in a coma? Had he been there as backup and somehow got caught up in the crossfire?

And why hadn't Ralph Chason reported the trespasser long before now? Maybe because he used that site to enjoy his stash of pot?

"Did you alert anyone about this man, Mr. Chason?"

Chason shook his head. "No, I didn't. I figured I'd scared him away. And then, all that commotion started—big machines digging dirt and construction crews in and out all the time. I quit going back there, but I'm still upset about it. I intend to build a big fence on that property line. I don't need tourists or vagrants traipsing all over my land."

Anderson stood to leave. "I might have to question you again, sir. But hopefully now we can find out who this man is and what he was doing back there."

"Well, you might start by doing an international criminal search," Chason said with confidence. "I watch enough crime shows to know that at least."

You and everyone else, Anderson thought. He tipped his hat. "Thanks. You take care."

"You, too," Chason said.

Then Anderson turned back. "I have one more question. Do you smoke pot?"

Chason's bushy eyebrows lifted. He hesitated, then shrugged. "I figure you pulled my record. You gonna bust me for that?"

"I should but I don't have any proof and I'm not here to find any right now. I did find part of a marijuana cigarette near a campsite on the property. Could that have been yours?"

Chason put his hands in the pockets of his baggy jeans. "Okay, all right. Yeah, it was mine. I've been back there a few times since the construction started. But I ain't done nothing except light up a joint, I swear."

Anderson wrote that in his notes. "Thanks for your cooperation. And as a reminder, you don't need another misdemeanor on your record, sir."

Chason waved a hand in the air. "I've heard it all, son. I know, I know. Point taken. I'm getting too old for all that sneaking around, anyway."

Anderson left, his gut feeling saying that Chason was telling the truth. Why would the man lie? He'd been pretty upfront about his dispute with Jennifer and about his enjoyment of a joint now and then. Of course, that could have been a smokescreen to hide his real purposes. For all Anderson knew, Chason was in cahoots with these criminals and was maybe being paid to keep his silence about what was back there. He could have been instructed to call in about the Irishman just to send Anderson on a wild-goose chase instead of watching that particular piece of property.

That would mean starting all over again from scratch. And it would also mean that Jennifer was still in a whole lot of danger.

THIRTEEN

Anderson pulled up to the alligator pond just in time to watch Boudreaux slide out of the open crate and take his first splash in the gray waters of the brand-new rock-encased pond.

Jennifer glanced up when he slammed his truck door but she waited for him, her hands on her hips, her expression questioning. "Where were you?"

"I'll tell you later," he said, careful because of all the people milling around. He scanned the woods and hills. "Everything go okay?"

She gave him an impatient look. "Just dandy. I've got to get back to work."

Was she mad that he'd left during the big event? Didn't the woman understand he had other fish to fry? Probably not, since her mind was solidly centered on these alligators and keeping them happy, even when her own safety was in question.

Anderson shook it off and glanced around, trying to gauge if any of the workers could be a drug runner or potential killer. But everyone looked focused and happy about the alligators finally having a new home. And he had to admit, since he'd continued his nightly stakeouts back here, things seemed to have settled down. Maybe the culprits had found what they were looking for the night of the fire. Or maybe Chason or someone else had tipped them off and deemed this place too hot right now.

But he was itching to know exactly what they'd tried so hard to get to, since it surely had a lot to do with the Lions.

His phone buzzed and he walked away from the activity inside the pond's chain-link fence to answer Ben's call.

"Still no luck on identifying the cóma patient," Ben said. "But I can't imagine why an Irishman is involved in this mess. Jimenez told us that almost all the cartel lackies are Mexican."

"Doesn't make a bit of sense. I really hope we're not going down the wrong road. What if the Lions had nothing to do with Greg's murder?"

Anderson watched as Bobby Wayne's big whip-like tail flipped in the air very near Jennifer's head. She got out of the way and the gator took off through the water.

Holding a long breath, he said, "What was he doing at Greg's house that day? Maybe he was hired for the hit but someone showed up and shot both of them. But who? And why shoot the hit man? We could be jumping to conclusions. He might not be a hit man. He could have been there for any number of reasons." He thought back over what Chason had said. "The neighbor did say the Irishman was arguing with someone on the phone. Maybe one of his cronies?"

"We need to find the answer to that," Ben replied.

"You keep watch on your side and we'll do the same here. I'm alerting the rest of the team on this in our meeting tomorrow morning. Meantime, I'll run a few more searches. Good work, Anderson."

Anderson clicked off then headed toward the crowd gathered around the pen. He had to admit, the place looked good. Two sets of chain-linked high-security fences kept the gators in and any inquisitive visitors out. The place had a swamp-like feel that included a weeping willow lapping into the pond on one end and some palm trees clustered behind several big sunning rocks on the other end. While the pond looked natural, the whole thing had been designed to give the alligators plenty of deep water on one side and lots of space to sun on the rocks and land all around it on the banks. There was a rock ledge with metal side rails that looked like a pier near one of the gates for keepers to feed the alligators either through the fence or with a pole. Nearby that, the small utility building, complete with a new circuit board, housed equipment, a refrigerator and treats for the alligators. It also now had a phone, and a small office and bathroom with a deep sink. The crew had finished up yesterday.

All around the perimeter, the woods glowed orange and yellow as the leaves of late fall continued to change. While the alligator habitat looked fresh and new against the pretty woods, Anderson couldn't help but wonder if someone was out there right now, watching and waiting.

His gut told him the cartel would strike again once things settled down.

"So what do you think?" Jennifer asked after she'd

made sure Boudreaux and Bobby Wayne were situated.

Anderson glanced at the spot where just two days ago, the earth had been lightly shoveled. Both he and Cade had decided to let things be for now, in hopes that whoever had been here would either return or that they'd found what they wanted and would make their next move somewhere else. He just wished he had discovered them in the process, but no use crying over spilled milk.

"I think those are two lucky alligators," he said since he didn't want to go into detail about his real concerns and feelings. "Now you can activate the security system we put in around the fence line."

"Yes." She gave him a level look. "That should keep anyone out from now on. I hope your drug runners will find a new place to do their dirty deeds. I want them to leave me alone."

"I hope I can catch them before they do anything else," he shot back. "But that doesn't mean you're safe, Jennifer."

"Yeah, right," she said, kicking mud off her boots. "I was harassed, attacked and my barn is toast. I think I'll remember that for a long time to come, Ranger-man."

"Well, maybe we can all sleep a little better tonight, at least."

She nodded. "I hear that. I'm exhausted. But my work is just beginning. Now I have to finish the rest of the updates and renovations around here, and somehow find a way to get the barn rebuilt and keep my animals fed and happy in the process. I hope to have a grand reopening around Christmas—a combination fundraiser and exposé. Then in the spring, we should be off and running for a long summer. That's our heaviest tourist season."

Anderson digested her heavy lineup, wondering how he could help ease her load. Then he thought of his mother. The woman could organize a committee in about five minutes, bake a casserole to feed everyone and have a project up and running before sundown. He'd have to give her a call later and solicit her help in getting some more volunteers and sponsors for Jennifer's compound. His mother had a wide circle of friends who loved to support causes like this. And due to the nature of his work, she wouldn't ask questions. She'd just go into action.

He looked up to find Jennifer watching him. "Uh-oh. I can see those wheels turning in your head. What's on your mind, Anderson?"

Amazed that she could read him so well, Anderson shrugged. No need to go into detail. He'd call his mom later. "Well, while I'm happy that this is one project you can mark as done, I'm also still on the case. And I'll be staked out back here for the next few days."

"You can't live on my property forever," she said, her eyes going wide in disbelief. "What are you hoping to find?"

"I don't know," he admitted. "They could be long gone or they could come back. I think somebody hid something back here and I'd like to catch that somebody digging up whatever it is—if it's still here."

She dug in her boots. "I won't allow any digging now that this is finished. It's too dangerous and it could ruin this carefully designed area."

"That's why I'm gonna be back here tonight and for the next few nights at least," Anderson tried to explain. "To catch them before they do any damage."

"Okay, right." She pushed at her long curls. "I'll be so glad when this is over and done."

"Me, too." But he sure didn't want things between them to be over and done. No, sir. And volunteering here on a regular basis would be one way for him to keep tabs on Jennifer.

"I've got some things to finish up here," Jennifer said, her tone dismissive. But she turned to face him again, hesitant now. "I'll see you back at the house."

Anderson nodded, then whirled to leave. He had a lot to do, anyway. Now that they had a lead on the coma victim, maybe they could find a break in this case.

And in the meantime, he'd give his mother a call about getting some help out here. That is, if Jennifer would accept that help, stubborn woman that she was.

Jennifer got up early the next morning to voices outside her door. Becky had gone back to the city, but the usual helpers were scheduled. She didn't recall having this many people on the roster for today.

After dressing and grabbing her coffee and a power bar, she headed outside to see what was going on.

And found about twenty people gathered around one tiny dark-haired woman.

"Excuse me," Jennifer said as she parted the crowd and turned to stare at everyone. "We're not open to the public right now due to renovations. How did y'all get in here?"

The tiny woman grinned and reached out her hand.

"Hi. You must be Jennifer. I'm Ramona Michaels, Anderson's mom. And this is Katie, his younger sister. And here's Blake and Derek, my other two sons."

The teen girl with long blond hair smiled shyly at her while the two Anderson-like brothers grinned and ribbed each other.

"Nice to meet you but what are you doing here?" Jennifer asked while Mrs. Michaels gave her a sturdy handshake. "Where's Anderson?"

"I can explain," Mrs. Michaels said. "He had to go to a meeting this morning, so he called me yesterday and told me about helping you out here and got me all excited about volunteering. He opened the gate for us. I corralled the whole family and a few friends to come and help. My husband, Andrew, is already down at the barn with several very experienced men, working on a plan to get things cleaned up and ready to rebuild."

"I can't do any reconstruction on the barn until I get clearance from the insurance company and they cut me a check," Jennifer said. "But I do appreciate the help."

And just wait until she saw Anderson Michaels. The man could have warned her or *asked* her, at least, before bringing in reinforcements.

"We won't mess that up," Mrs. Michaels replied, her brown eyes full of mirth. She tugged at her old University of Texas Longhorns sweatshirt. "But we *are* here to help out. Now I have us divided into three teams. You just tell us what needs to be done. We're here for the day and me and the other ladies from our Sensational Seniors group brought a picnic lunch to feed everyone."

Jennifer looked around at the eager, expectant faces,

tears pricking at her eyes. "I don't know what to say, except thanks, Mrs. Michaels."

"Call me Ramona," Anderson's perky little mother said, taking Jennifer by the arm. "Anderson told me you've had a tough time of things lately. He must think highly of you to volunteer like this." She leaned close and whispered, "That man lives for his work most days."

If you only knew, Jennifer thought. But she didn't have the heart to say anything bad about Anderson to his mother. "He's been an asset around here lately," she replied, thinking that was as close to the truth as she could allow for now.

Knowing his meeting must be about this case, she didn't dare ask his mother for any further information.

"I'll show you what needs to be done," she said, thinking of the leaves that needed raking and the shrubs and bushes that needed to be cleared. Now that the gators had a new home, Jennifer wanted to move some of the sea turtles she'd rescued from the gulf after a recent hurricane into the smaller watering hole near the main house. With all these willing people, she could probably get that done today, too. It would take her mind off the darkness and danger she felt at every turn.

"Okay," she said, her brain already organizing and compartmentalizing this added blessing. "Here's what I need done."

It didn't take long for the whole Michaels clan to dig in and get to work. By noon, Jennifer could understand where Anderson got his work ethic. His folks were nice, rowdy, loving and hardworking. A wonderful example of a good, solid Christian family.

Thinking she'd have to thank Anderson when she saw him, she couldn't be mad at the man. He'd done her a great service and it touched her heart. Most of the time, she only heard stories of her friends' families. Today, she'd been given a gift of actually seeing a loving family in action. Even while deeply engrossed in her work, Jennifer had stopped now and then to watch Anderson's two handsome younger brothers roughhousing with each other, their sister breaking them apart with a stern scolding that belied the twinkle in her pretty eyes. And she'd seen his mother taking charge with firm but pleasant suggestions and orders to everyone while his quiet father stood by, solidly backing his wife and adding his own advice.

She hated to see them leave at the end of the day.

Telling herself to be grateful for a gift from God, Jennifer didn't think past that. She refused to dream about being a part of Anderson's life.

No matter how wonderful his mother's no-meat lasagna had tasted at lunch.

Later that afternoon, Anderson waved goodbye to his folks and walked back up onto the porch to stand beside Jennifer. "You okay?" he asked, watching for signs of her stubbornness.

"I am now," she said, her gaze moving over the clean, spiffed-up compound. "I hadn't even noticed fall until today. Your family and friends did such a good job. I mean, look at those pumpkins they placed all around.

And the fresh haystacks, too. It makes me think of Thanksgiving and pumpkin pie."

She looked rested and content in spite of the long day's work and the things she'd been through over the last week.

"My mama gave me specific instructions to tell you that you're welcome at our place anytime. And I agree with her," Anderson said.

"I'll think about that later," she said, whirling to go inside. "After you crack this case and I know I can finally enjoy life again."

Anderson tugged her back around. "I told you about the lead we got on the guy in the coma. That's a big deal, Jennifer. I hope we'll soon have a name. It's the break we needed."

"But you still have to stake out the alligator pen, right?"

He nodded, his hands moving down her arms. "Yeah, for now. I just have a gut feeling these people aren't done back there." He tugged her close. "I can arrange for someone to stay here with you tonight."

"No, I'm a big girl, Anderson. You do what you need to do and I'll catch up on some paperwork. I'm exhausted, anyway."

He didn't want to leave her. "Okay. Let's get inside and eat the leftovers my mom saved for us, then I'll head out. You keep your phone nearby, okay?"

"Okay." She followed him inside and together they prepared the lasagna and salad Ramona had tucked inside the refrigerator. "Your mother made enough to feed half of Texas."

"She made enough for us to have a nice quiet dinner,"

Anderson replied. He bent down beside old Roscoe, petting the dog like he did every night before he left Jennifer and Roscoe to do his job. "Roscoe, you might like some leftovers, too."

"He's not getting any better," Jennifer said, coming to sit by the dog. "I hate watching him waste away but…I don't have the heart to let Dr. Jenkins put him to sleep. He assures me Roscoe's not in any pain."

"The old boy's just resting, I reckon," Anderson replied, his eyes gentle on hers. "He deserves a good long rest."

"Let's eat," she said, getting up to hurry back to the kitchen.

Anderson followed her, then turned her around to face him. "Are you sure you're okay?"

She bobbed her head, looking back at the dog. "I just…I don't know how to thank you or your family for what you did today. Your dad already has a construction crew lined up to rebuild the barn and your mother told me the women in her Sensational Seniors group are going to become permanent patrons for Rodgers Exotic Animal Rescue. The amount of their financial pledge is astonishing. How can I ever repay that?"

Anderson leaned close, then tucked a cluster of curls away from her face. "You don't have to." Then he bent and kissed her, something he'd wanted to do all day. "Consider it a gift."

When they parted, her eyes were rich with longing. "I think I owe you a lot of kisses for today, Anderson."

"Then pay up."

He kissed her again, wishing he could stay here instead of having to go out on patrol. But there was no help for it. He had to end this case so he could figure out what was going on between them.

The woman made his heart race with need and his mind whirl with possibilities. And he prayed that the example his family had shown her today would guide her back to the Lord.

"Let's eat," he said, "before I decide to let Boudreaux and Bobby Wayne take out the bad guys without me."

She smiled at that. "They could probably do just that, Ranger-man." Reaching up a hand to touch his face, she added, "Before we eat, there's something I need to say."

"All right." He waited, never able to read her.

"I know you have a strong faith," she said, her smile confirming her sincerity. "But today, I witnessed that faith firsthand. Your family is wonderful. They made me think long and hard about my bitterness toward God. I started thinking about that the first day you and I worked together and since then…I've felt this tugging in my heart. So I just wanted you to know, no matter what happens, I'll always be grateful for that."

Anderson's joy caused him to pull her close again. Hugging her, he kissed the top of her head. "Now that was worth the trip."

She stood back, laughing up at him. "You're something else, Ranger-man. Just be careful out there."

He intended to be careful. He had a very good reason to settle this fight now. He wouldn't give up until he knew she was safe. And then maybe he'd be able to figure out how to balance his work with his growing feelings for Jennifer.

FOURTEEN

Two nights later, Anderson lay on his bedroll, bundled under a thick wool blanket, watching the crescent moon nestled against the stars like a necklace and wondering if he was going to have to call it a day on this stakeout and get back to headquarters for another assignment.

Apparently, the drug cartel and the Lions had been spooked by the new developments and were now staying away. They'd either found what they'd wanted or they knew he was still around and so were avoiding the place. Either way, he was getting itchy and restless. Patience had never been his strong point, but this was driving him crazy.

Rather, being around Jennifer and not being able to act on his feelings was driving him crazy. A stolen kiss here and there wasn't nearly enough. He wanted to take her home to meet the family she'd already met and he wanted to keep her safe and he wanted to be able to come here on a regular basis in his off-hours and help her.

In a word, he wanted to spend time with the woman. Time that didn't involve danger lurking around the corner.

"I'm singing a new tune now, Mama. And you'd be so happy to hear that." But would Jennifer? And what about his policy regarding never getting personally involved in investigations? He'd need to finish this job before he could even begin to sort out his feelings.

If he ever got a chance to do that. Anderson shifted, careful to scope the whole pond area since another quiet hour had come and gone. He'd purposely waited until well past dark to come out here, walking on foot this time so he wouldn't alert anyone who might chance by.

It was past midnight and still not a peep, not even from those two sneaky alligators. Anderson closed his eyes, his mind going over and over the variables of this case.

He must have dozed because the next thing he knew, he heard a grunt and then what sounded like a shovel hitting dirt.

And it was coming from *inside* the alligator pond.

Jennifer heard the loud beep of the alarm system, the faraway fog of sleep muting the alert. But within moments she was up and running toward the security control box located next to her computer in the front office, her feet bare, her heart pumping.

With one quick glance, she saw that the alert was coming from the alligator pond.

Anderson was out there! And someone was trying to break in?

Whirling, she started back toward the gun closet, intent on going to help Anderson, when a strong arm caught her and a sweaty hand covered her mouth.

"Don't try anything, lady, or you die."

She struggled, but the man held her tight. "We warned you but you wouldn't listen. We can't let you live now."

What did that mean? Were they going to kill her just because she'd infringed on their meeting place? Or because she had seen one of them up close? Trapped, Jennifer held her breath while she frantically glanced around for some sort of weapon.

And then the weapon she'd never expected came lunging out of the darkness, surprising both the intruder and Jennifer.

Roscoe barked and growled. Jennifer scrambled against her attacker, then using all the strength she could muster, planted her bare foot against the man's sneaker.

That didn't work so well. And now, Roscoe was up and snarling at the man's pant leg.

The man shouted at the dog, turning with Jennifer, his hand still over her mouth, to kick at Roscoe. But Roscoe wouldn't let up. He barked and growled, biting and leaping away from the man's vicious assault.

Jennifer twisted enough to get a good look at the man's face, her pulse striking against her temple as she realized he looked like the invader from the barn. Then she found just enough space to elbow the man in the ribs at the same time Roscoe latched on to his leg.

The attacker let Jennifer go, then tried with all his might to get Roscoe off him, the hood covering his long dark hair falling away to reveal a dark mustache and startled, sinister eyes. Jennifer watched in horror as the man spun around, dragging a fighting-mad Roscoe around the room.

Looking for a weapon, Jennifer picked up an old gray metal first-aid kit she'd refilled earlier and left on the counter. Waiting for the man to turn away, she rushed toward him and whacked him on the top of his stringy hair, right in the center of his head.

The man went down with another grunt and fell inside the office.

And then Roscoe let go and fell down just outside the office door.

Anderson dragged himself belly-style toward the dark-dressed man inside the alligator compound, watching as the man took off his heavy jacket and went to work digging. The silent alarm should have sounded at the house so he got out his phone and put in a call to Jennifer.

She didn't pick up.

Praying she'd stay put and not come rushing in to protect those two snarly alligators, Anderson slid closer and closer to the spot in the first chain-link where the intruder had obviously cut the wiring. Same thing with the second shorter fence inside the pond. The cuts had set off the alarm, but the man now frantically digging on the dirt-packed shoreline at the shallow end of the pool didn't know he'd triggered that alarm.

And he apparently didn't know or care that two mean alligators were within feet of where he was busy working.

Anderson watched the man then tried to call Jennifer again. Still no answer. He'd have to act fast to subdue this intruder, then hurry to check on Jennifer. He lifted up, his rifle scoped on the dark figure tossing sand and dirt in all directions, inches from the murky waters of the pond. The man was making enough noise to alert the whole countryside.

"Hold it right there," Anderson said, calling out to the man. "Texas Ranger. Put your hands up where I can see them. Now."

The intruder turned in surprise, dropping his shovel into the shallow water with a loud clatter and a heavy splash, his hands going up as he squinted into the moonlight.

Anderson knew his kind. The man would try to run and Anderson would have to make the choice of shooting him or chasing him. Either way, this was going to be a long night.

But then, everything changed. The man looked at Anderson, trying to gauge his chances and started to turn. But a quick splash in the water near him caused him to spin around.

And then Anderson watched as the younger, smaller of the gators, Bobby Wayne, slid with lightning speed up onto the shallow sand and rocks and snapped and snarled at the man's foot, his eerie war cry shattering the night.

The man screamed out in fear and managed to get away, his feet slipping and sliding, his pant leg tearing as he ran up over a jutting rock. Bobby Wayne advanced, still hissing his anger, his big tail flapping against the wet rocks.

"Stay right there," Anderson called, heading around the fence line to try and block the man.

But the man took that as his chance to get away. When Bobby Wayne came closer, the intruder screamed and took off running, then ducked through the cut in the fence.

Even though Anderson fired a couple of rounds, the man never looked back. Anderson hurried after him, running as fast as he could to catch the man who'd pushed through the jagged tear in the outer fence on the other side of the pond.

He heard an engine crank up and figured the man had hidden some sort of motorbike or off-road vehicle in the woods. Even if Anderson called for backup, it would be too late to get anyone out here now. The alarm should have alerted Jennifer, though.

He'd lost the intruder. And he had to check on Jennifer.

Aggravated, he turned around to make sure the man hadn't doubled back.

And came face-to-face with a snarling alligator coming toward the open cut in the security fence.

Anderson had to act quickly. He hurried to the outside gate and grunted with each twist of the heavy metal wires as he tried with all his might to string the torn gate back together. He'd just finished the last twist when Bobby Wayne hissed and lunged toward the gate.

But the wires held and Anderson breathed a sigh of relief. "I should have let you have at him," he told the mean, mad alligator. Picking up a rock, Anderson tossed it beyond Bobby Wayne. It made a splash in the water behind the gator. Bobby Wayne whirled and took off to investigate.

Then Anderson's cell buzzed.

Jennifer. "Are you all right?" he asked into the phone.

"Anderson, I need you to come back, right now." Then she hung up.

But the low, shaking tone of her words scared Anderson even more than witnessing a man almost getting eaten alive by an alligator.

He found her sitting with a chair wedged against the door into the front office, Roscoe in her lap, tears streaming down her face as she rocked back and forth.

"Jennifer?" Anderson glanced around. There had been a struggle here. "Jennifer?" he said, loudly this time. "Are you all right?"

She shook her head then talked fast, her voice lifting, sobs halting her words. "A man. He attacked me. I hit him over the head but…Roscoe came after him." She looked up, searching. "I was so worried about Roscoe— I shut off the office. That's where they fell, both of them. I dragged Roscoe inside here. I think the man got up and ran out the door when he heard me on the phone."

"Did you get a look at him?"

She nodded. "I saw his face. I saw him, Anderson. It was the same man who came after me in the barn."

"I'll be right back," Anderson said. He moved the chair away and hurried to the front of the building. No sign of the intruder inside the building and no sign of a getaway car outside. Another diversion that had gone wrong?

He didn't have time to analyze that now. He rushed back to Jennifer. "He's not in there. How's Roscoe?"

She looked up at him with watery eyes then looked back down at the dog, sobs shaking her shoulders. "I think he's...he's gone, Anderson. He saved my life and now...he's just gone."

Anderson felt around on the dog, moving his fingers over Roscoe's neck and chest. No pulse.

His heart breaking, Anderson reached for Jennifer. "C'mon now, honey. Let me help you up."

"No," she said, pulling away, her arms holding tightly to the big unmoving dog. "I can't...I can't let him go, Anderson. I can't. It's always been just him and me. How can I ever let him go?"

Anderson wasn't sure how to answer that question. He had two intruders out there on the run and a breach in the security at the alligator pond. And a half-dug dirt hole gaping near those gators.

But right now, he had an inconsolable, hurting woman refusing to let go of the dog she loved with all her heart.

"Hold on," he told Jennifer. "Just sit right there with Roscoe. We're gonna make it all right, Jennifer, I promise."

It was time to call in backup. First, he called 911 to report the break-ins.

Then he hit speed dial on his phone and waited for a voice on the other end. "I need you. Yeah, something's happened at the rescue farm. Can you come?"

"I'll be right there," his mother said on the other end of the line.

* * *

Jennifer sat on the couch beside a warm fire, a cup of hot tea in her hand. But she couldn't move. She couldn't function.

Anderson's mother came to sit beside her. "How you doing, suga'?"

Jennifer glanced up, her eyes so swollen it was hard to focus. "I'm okay," she said, too numb to admit that she was slowly falling apart. "Where's Anderson?"

Ramona shook her head. "Out there by the alligator pond with a couple of Rangers and the sheriff. I don't know the particulars of why he's called in everybody, but from the look of things, he's found something back there. Something bad enough to bring in several other lawmen." Ramona reached out to touch Jennifer's hand. "He's been working on this case for a while, hasn't he, honey?"

Jennifer bobbed her head. "Yes, ma'am. I wasn't supposed to say anything."

Ramona gave her a wan smile. "It's okay. He gave me a vague sense of what was going on. I live with that day and night. When that phone rang earlier, I tell you, my heart went straight to my feet. I thought, this is it, Lord. The call I've always dreaded."

Jennifer's whole system jolted back to life. "I'm sorry. I…I've never considered that you'd have to deal with that, too. How do you live with the constant worry and fear?"

"It's not easy," Ramona said, "but Anderson is smart and he's good at what he does. Right now, he's just hurting 'cause he wasn't here for you tonight. Duty first and all that stuff."

"But he was here," Jennifer said, tears misting over in her eyes again. "He was here when I needed him the most." She glanced toward Roscoe's empty bed by the fireplace.

Earlier, Anderson helped her up to the sofa, then he silently and gently carried Roscoe into another room, returning to the den to find Roscoe's favorite blanket. Without a word, he went back to Roscoe and covered the big animal. Then he shut the door to the laundry room.

"We'll bury him in the morning," he told Jennifer.

And after that, he'd gathered her in his arms and held her while she cried out all her pain from her parents' divorce, her dad's death, her mother's grief and distance, Roscoe's courage…and her own relationship with the Lord.

Anderson had put her first, ahead of the bad guys out there. Ahead of his job. He'd stayed with her when she needed someone to just be there. And because he'd held her and comforted her, Jennifer knew she'd never be the same.

"He was here," she said again now, wiping at her eyes. "And because he was here, my life has changed… so much."

Ramona gave her a long, measuring look. "I think his has, too, sweetie. I sure think his has, too."

Then Ramona got up and pulled the sunflower afghan off the back of the couch. "Why don't you lie down and just shut your eyes. You don't have to sleep. Just rest."

Jennifer slid down onto the old couch and let

Anderson's mother cover her, the warmth of the blanket almost as welcome as the warmth of Ramona's soft hands on her wet cheeks.

"Just rest now. We'll be here when you wake up."

Jennifer closed her eyes, her misery over losing Roscoe tempered with the blessing of having someone to wake up to. At long last.

FIFTEEN

It had been a grisly discovery. First, Anderson and Cade found a dirty denim jacket that the trespasser had left, and in the pocket of that jacket, a business card with an interesting name—Senator Frederick Huffington, President Pro Tem of the Texas Senate.

That alone was a major find, until Anderson had kicked around in the unearthed dirt and hit on something hard inside the two-foot deep hole.

And it looked like a human skull.

'A team had been called in, complete with cadaver dogs, to find the evidence that had caused a man to risk his life in order to dig back here. And they'd found it, all right. A body, buried in a shallow grave underneath a few heavy rocks that had been so natural-looking, Jennifer and the construction team hadn't even moved them when they were redoing this area. But the late-night digger had moved them in a desperate search for the body.

Now, Anderson watched as the medical examiner and his team carefully exhumed the human skeleton, complete with rotting clothes.

Murder was sure a strong enough motive for the

Lions and their cohorts to try and get to that body before anyone else discovered it. And a strong motive for them to try and get to Jennifer Rodgers, to keep her from finding the body and stop her from identifying anyone.

Last night, in a final attempt to take out any possible witnesses, they'd come after her. And she'd seen the face of her attacker. She could still be in danger.

When Anderson considered what could have happened, he had to grit his teeth. And thank God that he'd been sent here in time.

Now Anderson and Cade Jarvis waited for the ME to give them a report. Since Cade was the assigned UCIT Ranger in their company, he'd take over with the unidentified body and make sure it got to the crime lab. The Rangers' Unsolved Crime Investigative Team used to be just that—a team. Now most companies were assigned one man, which meant Cade was sometimes stretched pretty thin.

And it looked like now was one of those times.

"They murdered someone and buried the body back here. That puts a whole new wrinkle on things," Anderson said, turning as another vehicle rolled up and parked. It was their fellow Ranger, Oliver Drew.

"Looks like Ben sent in reinforcements," Cade said with a shrug and a nod toward Drew. "He wanted someone besides you to take Jennifer's statement."

They waited while Oliver sauntered up, took a look at the activity, then glanced back at them. "Morning, boys."

"How'd it go with Jennifer?" Anderson asked, thinking Ben would yank him off the case if he kept showing too much interest in Jennifer Rodgers.

Oliver stared at the human bones in the open earth. "She gave me a pretty good description of her attacker. If I don't get any hits based on what she told me, you might need to bring her in to look at some mug shots or maybe a lineup."

"Okay." Lifting his chin toward the ME, Anderson updated Oliver. "Doc there says from what he can tell on the initial exam, male with a possible gunshot wound through the torso. What's left of the clothes indicate he was wearing a fancy sportscoat and possibly wool trousers. Doc there recognized what's left of the labels—not the kind an illegal would be wearing."

Oliver lifted his eyebrows. "Think it's the cartel's work?"

"I'd say so," Anderson retorted, on edge and exhausted from being up all night. "Since I caught someone digging in this spot in the middle of the night, I'd say that's a sure bet. They used every trick in the book to keep Jennifer from continuing work back here, including distracting her and me both by burning down the barn and attacking her last night. The deceased could have been involved with the Lions. I think they were concerned about being monitored by these cameras that weren't working until recently."

Oliver put his hands on his hips, his sunglasses shadowing his eyes. "Suspect got away?"

Anderson nodded. "Hispanic from what I could tell. He screamed out and jabbered a whole slew of foul words—in Spanish."

"At you?" Oliver asked with a twisted grin.

"No." Anderson pointed to where he and some other men had tugged some chicken wire across the shallow end of the pond. "At those two mean gators staring at us."

Oliver jumped and turned around. "Man, you should have told me that before I got so close to that wire."

Cade shook his head. "Relax, Anderson got some zoo expert out here to help since Miss Rodgers is pretty shook up about all of this. We're safe for now, aren't we, Anderson?"

"I hope so," Anderson replied, eyeing the makeshift skirting, memories of holding Jennifer while she cried still fresh in his mind. Thank goodness his mother and some of the other volunteers had convinced her to stay away from this mess. "Just long enough to clear the crime scene."

Cade squinted into the water. "You'd think the man might have noticed he was in danger, what with the signs everywhere."

"It was dark and I don't think he was as worried about Boudreaux and Bobby Wayne as he was about finding this body and getting it out of here. I guess I should name Bobby Wayne an official member of our team now, even if he did scare the man away."

Oliver snorted, then glanced back toward where the crime scene team went about their work. "Any idea on the identity?"

"No, nothing yet on the body or what remains of the clothes, but Anderson did find a jacket the intruder left, and a business card inside the pocket," Cade replied. "Doc says he's pretty sure the deceased was male. I'm escorting the body to the lab in San Antonio."

Anderson held up the plastic-encased business card.

"Senator Frederick Huffington. Still can't figure why the perp had the good senator's card on him."

Cade looked over at Oliver. "Doesn't make a whole lot of sense, does it?"

Oliver glanced around, then tugged on his hat. "Nothing about this case makes any sense. A senator's card, an Irishman in a coma. I tell you, boys, some days are just more interesting than others." After staring down at the gruesome scene, he finally said, "Gotta go."

Anderson waved him away. "Thanks for helping out."

After Oliver drove away, Anderson and Cade turned their attention back to the task at hand. "I need to check on Jennifer," Anderson said, glancing at his watch. "Hopefully, between her regular volunteers and my formidable mama, she listened and let someone else do all the work around here for a change."

She needed to be out there, tending to her animals.

Instead, Jennifer was stuck in the house with well-meaning people hovering around. She'd tried to sleep but that hadn't worked. She kept seeing a dark-haired man coming toward her in the muted darkness. She kept seeing Roscoe leaping up to protect her.

And she couldn't get past the image of her sweet old dog lying silent and still in her arms or the way Anderson had taken over, making things better, holding her, letting her cry her heart out while he wrapped her in his solid warmth. He even called the vet to come take Roscoe for the night. They'd bury him tomorrow.

Now, Anderson and all kind of law enforcement people were swarming around her property because they'd found a body buried by the new alligator pond.

Jennifer shuddered, thinking of all the times she'd walked near those jagged rocks, of the times she'd sat on those very same rocks, watching the crew work. She'd gone back there by herself time and time again. Thinking about it now made her queasy.

Who had died back there? What kind of torment had they suffered at the hands of these dangerous, evil people?

Feeling antsy, Jennifer got up to stare out the window. Jacob stood speaking to a group of volunteers. Ramona Michaels was busy washing out the old alligator pen in preparation for moving the sea turtles to that area.

Life went on, even though Jennifer was caught in a spiderweb of pain and grief. Without thinking of it, she reached for the phone. Her mother had loved Roscoe as much as she did. Did she dare call Suzanne and tell her about Roscoe?

Jennifer closed her eyes and sent up a prayer for guidance. Anderson had changed her, his presence and his deep faith had shown Jennifer that maybe she'd held on to her grief and bitterness for too long. And life was too short to hold grudges or turn her back on her mother. So she opened her eyes and dialed Suzanne's number, her heart shifting and pumping with anticipation and fear.

Would her mother even answer her calls?

"Hello?"

Jennifer gulped, swallowed. "Mom?"

"Jenny? Is that you?"

"It's me. How are you?"

"I'm okay. How about you?"

Jennifer pushed at the lump forming in her throat, fought against the hot tears. "I'm…not so good, Mom. Roscoe died this morning. And…vandals have been harassing me. I don't know anymore. I don't think I can do this. I want to hold on to this place but things aren't looking so great right now."

She heard her mother inhale, then go silent. "I'll be there as soon as I can book a flight home, honey."

Jennifer hung up, tears falling freely down her face now. It had taken everything in her to make that phone call, but it had paid off. Her mother was coming home.

She turned, wiping at her eyes, and found Anderson standing in the door from the office. Without a word, she rushed into his arms. He pulled her close, kissing the top of her hair.

"How you doing?"

She drew back, wiping at her eyes. "Better. I…I called my mother. She's coming home."

He shot her a surprised, bittersweet smile. "That's good. You'll need her now."

She looked up and saw the hope in his eyes. "I do need her. And I've been so stubborn, I didn't see that. I didn't know how to ask, Anderson. But when you called your mother to come here and help me—"

"It made you want your own mother, right?"

She bobbed her head. "I thought I didn't need anyone, not even God. But I was so wrong."

Anderson leaned down to give her a quick kiss. "You're gonna be fine. You have a lot of support now."

She wanted to ask if that included him, but she didn't

have to. She could see that in his expression, in the way his cat-like golden eyes washed her in a shimmering warmth.

"I'm blessed." She put her head on his shoulder, savoring the scent of his old suede jacket mixed with evergreen and outdoors. "I'll just miss Roscoe so much."

"I know, darlin'. It's hard to let go of a faithful companion." He lifted her, a finger on her chin. "But, you have a new faithful companion now. You have me, Jennifer. For as long as you want me around."

Jennifer didn't know how to respond to that declaration. She wanted him around for a very long time, but her heart was still fragile and bruised. "Thank you," she said. "Thank you, Anderson, for everything."

He drew back, confusion clouding his eyes. "We'll talk later. I've got to get back to it."

Knowing she hadn't been completely honest with him, Jennifer followed him to the back door. "Is the… body gone now?"

"Yes. On its way to Austin. Cade's taking over since he's our unsolved crime expert. It's gonna be hard to ID the body since we didn't find any means of identification on the corpse. But if anyone can figure it out, Cade will." He studied her face for a long time. "I know you want to get back to work, but you need to rest—just for today. And…tomorrow, I have to go into Austin to talk to someone regarding this case. If you feel like riding along, we could have lunch in the city."

Jennifer shook her head. "I have a lot of work—"

"Call in that zoo expert who helps you out now and then. Call in your volunteers and Doc Jenkins. You need to get away from here for a while, Jennifer. It's still not safe for you."

"You mean because I saw that man's face?"

"Yes. I want to keep you close. He could come back."

The thought of that riled her out of her grief. "My mom's coming in but I'm not sure when she'll arrive. I won't be alone."

"I'd still feel better if you were with me in the city."

She didn't miss the authority in his words. "I thought this was over."

"We're getting there. And you can help while we're at it. Would you mind looking at some rap sheets to see if you can identify your attacker?"

The last thing she wanted to do. "If it means an end to this, I'll be glad to."

He gave her one last look. "This will be over soon. Then you can get back to doing what you love."

Jennifer wanted to shout out the truth, that she'd fallen for him and she'd never be the same again. She'd come a long way. Anderson had brought her back to her faith and her mother was coming home. It was a start. The last step would be in giving her heart over to Anderson without any doubts or qualms.

And she couldn't do that until this shadow of danger was no longer hanging over her head. Because not until then would she find out if Anderson was only here because of his job and the rush of catching bad guys. Or if he was willing to stick around for her, as he'd promised, after the danger was over.

SIXTEEN

Anderson sat around the big conference table with his fellow Rangers, listening while Captain Ben Fritz updated them on the latest findings of the case. Senior Captain Doug Parker stood by, tugging at his handlebar mustache.

"Thanks to Anderson's diligence in trying to see what the cartel and the Lions were doing on the property owned by Jennifer Rodgers of Rodgers Exotic Animal Rescue Farm, we have some new developments in this case." Ben nodded toward Anderson. "Good work, Ranger Michaels."

Anderson lifted a finger in response.

Ben went over the particulars, giving timelines as he went. "After putting out an urgent call about a developing case, our captain Gregory Pike was murdered in his home in September. An unconscious man was also found at the scene and still remains in a coma at the hospital in San Antonio. After attempts to identify him failed, photos of this man were circulated and a witness identified him as being Irish. More on that later.

"Eddie Jimenez, lower-level member of an organization called the Lions of Texas, remains in custody after the attempted murder of Corinna Pike." He glanced down briefly, then continued. "Jimenez refuses to give up the goods on the cartel or the Lions, but he did confess about a drop site located in the woods behind Rodgers Exotic Animal Rescue Farm. Ranger Anderson Michaels went undercover on the farm where so far, we've had a break-in in the tack room but no solid evidence to connect to the Lions or the cartel, a shed was vandalized and electrical equipment destroyed, attacks on Miss Rodgers just outside the barn and later inside her home, and a fire deliberately set in the barn as a diversion because of heavy activity where Miss Rodgers built a new alligator pond on property she purchased after her father died. Possible motive—they think her security cameras captured their activities back there.

"The seller of the property is clean but Miss Rodgers is also dealing with a disgruntled neighbor, one Ralph Chason, who doesn't want the alligators on that particular spot. However, he has an alibi for the times of the break-in, attacks and the fire but he has admitted to spending time on that piece of property. Meanwhile, we circulated a photo of the man in a coma and Chason returned from a business trip, saw the photo and called it in, saying he's seen the man. Based on the information given by Chason we know that the man is Irish. We're continuing to search for his identity, but he's still in a coma."

Ben looked at Anderson. "In the meantime, Jennifer Rodgers was attacked in her home by an intruder who told her she has to die. Miss Rodgers gave a description of the intruder and is willing to look over mug shots and rap sheets in order to identify him. That brings us to the latest findings—the skeletal remains found at the farm. Ranger Cade Jarvis is in charge of possibly bringing in forensic artist Paige Bryant to help with identifying the deceased."

Anderson held up the business card he'd found in the discarded jacket. "Suspect left his jacket, which will be checked for DNA and fiber evidence. Senator Frederick Huffington's business card was inside the right front pocket. I've been assigned to interview the senator to see if he can shed some light on this. However, he's out of town for a couple of days. Unavailable." Conveniently unavailable the way Anderson saw it.

Anderson glanced around at the people present— Senior Captain Parker, Captain Fritz, Cade Jarvis, Oliver Drew, Daniel Boone Riley, the lone woman in the group—Gisella Hernandez and Levi McDonnell, along with Trevor Donovan, Marvel Jones and Evan Chen. "Any suggestions on that card?"

"Why would a senator give his card to a possible illegal?" Gisella asked, her dark eyes widening.

"Maybe he's working an angle, hoping to get votes in the future," Levi called out.

"He just happened to be at a rally and the suspect got his card off a table?" Oliver suggested.

"Anderson will have to look into that when the good senator returns," Ben said. "The other part of this puzzle is the Irishman. Why and how did an Irishman end up camping out on the rescue farm land? Are the Lions using him for his connections and his expertise in criminal activities or did he just happen upon that land? We do have an eyewitness—Ralph Chason said he definitely saw the Irishman back there, arguing with someone on a cell phone."

"Obviously, the Irishman was there to meet up with the cartel and the Lions," Daniel Riley replied. "He might know about the body, too. And that might explain why he's in a coma now."

The talk went on with everyone speculating as they went over the evidence and the facts again.

Finally, Ben held up a hand. "Hopefully, after Cade consults Paige Bryant, we can identify the body—not much else we can do on that for now. The dental records did not produce a match. And since we don't have a name for the Irishman, until he wakes up, we're at a standstill there. Right now, I want Anderson to focus on the senator. Levi, you go with him. We'll meet again in a few days for any updates."

Levi nodded toward Anderson. "Got it."

Anderson lifted a hand. "And about the threat we got regarding the Alamo celebration, Daniel and I will work together to assure the committee we will investigate any and all threats."

Senior Captain Parker looked at Anderson. "FYI, Sam Myers is a member of the Alamo Planning Committee."

"Sam Myers?" Anderson went on high alert. "He's Jennifer Rodgers's grandfather."

Ben let out a grunt. "We put that together after you mentioned him being related to her. Wonder if the Lions have made the connection?"

"They're estranged and don't associate," Anderson said. "But this adds a new twist to our case."

"My daddy was good friends with Sam Myers and

several other members of that committee," Daniel Riley said.

Senior Captain Parker nodded. "When you two meet with the committee, maybe bring up the fact that his granddaughter is involved in this current situation. Might be able to pull some strings and get us some extra help."

Or, Anderson thought with renewed hope, this might help bring Jennifer and her grandparents together again and at least allow some good out of everything Jennifer had been through. It was worth a shot to mention this to Mr. Myers for that reason alone.

Jennifer rushed to the door to find her mother standing there. "Mom."

Her mother looked the same. Her golden brown hair styled in a shag, a scarf slung around her neck, slim jeans and dangling earrings and matching bracelet.

Suzanne took her daughter in her arms and hugged her tight. "I'm so sorry about Roscoe, baby."

Jennifer stood back, her smile belying her aching heart. "He was so old and he'd gone down over the last year or so. Doc Jenkins tried to help him but honestly, there wasn't much we could do. He made one last effort to protect me…and then, it was over."

Suzanne glanced around, her spiked hair falling around her cheekbones. "What do you mean, protect you? When you mentioned vandals, I didn't realize someone had tried to actually hurt *you*."

Jennifer didn't know where to begin. Since news of the body found on her property had been all over the television and papers, she supposed she could talk to her mother about things. She'd certainly had to calm down some of her patrons and supporters all day long. "Come on in and get settled," she said. "I'll explain everything."

An hour later, Suzanne stood out on the back porch, her shawl pulled around her shoulders as she stared out at the compound. "You've done a good job here, Jen. I should have stayed after your father died and helped but…this place brings back so many memories. Too many memories. I never stopped to consider you have to live with that every day, too."

Jennifer was glad to have her mother back but she was stronger now. She'd explain exactly how bad things had been at times. And she'd also had to explain the sheriff's deputy hovering around the property while Anderson was away.

But right now, she wanted to savor this moment of quiet beauty. Dusk was settling in a rich burnished sheen over the hills and woods. Anderson had been at a meeting in San Antonio headquarters all afternoon, and most of the volunteers and helpers were gone for the day. Even Anderson's mother had called it a day, telling Jennifer she'd be back in a couple of days to check on her.

"It's okay, Mom. It's been hard, but it's getting better. Once we have clearance and the gator pond is no longer a crime scene, I'll get it back in shape and start all over again."

"But, honey, the barn needs rebuilding, too. How can you cope with all of this? And why didn't you call me sooner? Break-ins, fires, a dead body. It's so scary. You should have called."

Jennifer wondered that herself. How could she answer? When they heard a truck rumbling up the driveway, she breathed a long sigh of relief.

"Is that your Ranger?" Suzanne asked with renewed interest as she craned her neck to see who was getting out of the truck.

Jennifer took a deep breath. "Yes, that's Anderson." Her mother had guessed about how close they'd become. No sense in trying to hide it. The relief that washed over Jennifer at seeing him emerge from the truck had to be evident all over her face.

"Hi," he said, glancing from Jennifer to her mother. Reaching out a hand, he took off his hat and said, "I'm Anderson Michaels."

"Suzanne Rodgers," her mom replied. "I've heard quite a lot about you, Mr. Michaels."

"It's Anderson, ma'am," he replied. Then he winked at Jennifer. "I'm sure it's all good, right?"

"Seems to be," Suzanne said, giving him an appraising look. "So far, at least."

Jennifer mustered a smile. "Your mother left a casserole—King Ranch chicken, I think. Actually, she made two—one with meat and one without."

"One of her best dishes and from a very famous recipe," Anderson replied. "I'm starved, too. But I want the one with chicken. No vegetarian-style for me."

The teasing look he gave Jennifer made her weak inside. But she tried to maintain her distance since her mother was watching them like a hawk. "I'll heat things up and we can talk over dinner. I want to know what happens next, Anderson."

"Yeah, me, too," he retorted. But she was pretty sure he wasn't talking about the case.

After dinner, Anderson and Suzanne sat down on the couch while Jennifer fixed a coffee tray and promised them "organic" cookies.

Taking this opportunity to talk to her mother in private, Anderson cleared his throat. "Mrs. Rodgers, I believe in full disclosure. And I have to tell you that I've been in touch with your father, Samuel Myers."

"Why?" Suzanne asked, sitting straight up. "You didn't call him about all this trouble here at the rescue center, did you?"

"No, ma'am, not exactly." Anderson explained the situation. "He's on a committee of bigwigs planning a celebration this summer for the 175th anniversary of the Battle of the Alamo. It's in regard to that—routine concerns with crowd control, things like that." No need to scare the woman with the details. "It's just that Jennifer could use some help around here and I thought maybe if your parents were aware of what she's trying to do—"

"That they'd help out, financially?" Suzanne asked, her pretty hazel eyes brightening. Then she leaned forward. "I have to admit, I've had the same thought. We've all been stubborn about this—and I've avoided them all these years out of pride. But now, Martin is gone and he left this legacy with his daughter, a blessing but certainly a challenge, too." She sat back, her hands twisted together. "I don't know how Jennifer would react. I purposely kept her away from my demanding parents so she could be her own person, not a socialite clone of some sort." Her shrug caused the shawl to fall down her arm. "I could have been wrong on that for so many reasons."

Anderson glanced toward the kitchen, then whispered, "Maybe together, we can figure out how to handle this. It might be an answer to my prayers."

Suzanne smiled. "You've been praying for my daughter?"

"Every waking hour since I met her, yes, ma'am."

When they heard Jennifer coming back, Suzanne gave him a quick smile. "Then I'd say your prayers have been answered. I think it's time I got my family back together. And knowing that you feel the same is a sure sign, I think. I can see that."

Anderson tipped his chin in agreement. Then he looked up and smiled at Jennifer. "Please tell me those cookies don't taste like cardboard, darlin'."

She shot him a frown. "Organic doesn't mean they'll taste bad. They were made with all natural ingredients that did no harm to animals. I think you'll approve."

Anderson wondered about that, but he did approve of her mother being here. Jennifer's mood had certainly changed and for that, he was grateful.

Now if he could find the man who'd attacked Jennifer, the threats to her would finally be over. He hoped.

SEVENTEEN

"Honey, the morning feedings are all finished so you go on into Austin with Anderson. You're allowed to take a day off now and then and this is important."

Jennifer looked at her mother, not so sure about Suzanne's advice. Her mother had been here two whole days and already Jennifer could sense that this time Suzanne meant business. Suzanne had been waiting early the morning after she arrived to go with Jennifer and Anderson to bury Roscoe.

With a peach-colored dawn rising and a sweet mist of dew covering the crimson and deep yellow trees and woods, Anderson had carried Roscoe's carefully wrapped body down a hill between the house and the barn, to be buried underneath a towering live oak.

"It was one of his favorite spots," Jennifer told her mother and Anderson after they'd buried the big dog.

Anderson had placed rocks over the grave and Suzanne set a pot of glistening burgundy and yellow mums against the tree's broad trunk. "Just until we can get him a proper headstone made."

Later, she'd insisted on helping Jennifer and Anderson with the feedings, especially the horses. Anderson had discreetly excused himself to do some paperwork, leaving mother and daughter alone in the stables, where a temporary wall had been built between the gutted barn and what was left of the horse stalls. It had been nice to spend a few hours with her mother, working side by side just like the old days.

Having her mother here helped with her grief over losing Roscoe. While she mourned the loss of her old friend, Jennifer knew enough about animals to understand Roscoe had been ready to go. So she tried to block out how he'd died and instead thanked God that Roscoe had been in her life and had come to her rescue in such a valiant way.

Going into Austin to the main Ranger headquarters located inside the Texas Department of Public Safety to look at mug shots of criminals would sure take her mind off her grief.

Suzanne tapped her on the hand. "Jenny, you've had a rough time of it lately. You need a break. You hear? I know this trip won't be pleasant but at least you'll get away from this place for a while."

Jennifer handed her mother a glass of water, then leaned back against the kitchen counter. "But you got here a few days ago and I didn't work yesterday. I'll be even more behind if I take today off, too."

Suzanne straightened her floral scarf around her neck, her eyes on Jennifer. "I can do your job. I still remember how things work around here. Jacob will be here at his regular time and the morning volunteers are already busy doing their chores. Becky even called and said she'd ride over after she gets off work, so the whole day is covered. Go with Anderson and do what needs to be done. I'll fix a light supper for y'all and Becky, so you can visit with her, too. That way you and Anderson can go over things in private and figure out how to put all of this behind you."

Jennifer didn't relish going over mug shots, but the sooner she got that done, the closer they'd be to ending this. Anderson had been in and out the last couple of days, tying up loose ends and filing reports. Maybe if they got away from the compound, they could both examine their feelings for each other. After everything that had happened, she wasn't sure what she was feeling. They could at least go back over the details of this case.

"Are you sure you don't mind, Mom?"

"I told you I don't," Suzanne replied. "I'm not going anywhere in a hurry, so we'll have plenty of time to catch up."

Jennifer paced the floor for a minute, then whirled. "Okay. But only because I want this to be over and done. I don't want you or my volunteers in danger."

Suzanne shuffled some papers on the desk. "I wish I'd been here with you."

"It's okay," Jennifer said, taking her mother's hand in hers. "You came when I called and that's important to me." Then she lowered her head. "I should have called you more."

Suzanne pulled her close. "Oh, honey, me, too. I've been so selfish. I know we kept in touch, but we never really talked about the kind of things mothers and daughters need to talk about." She stood back, wiping at her eyes. "Now that's enough. I'm here and things are gonna change. Go put on a pretty dress and try to have some fun after you visit the Ranger office, okay?"

Jennifer didn't waste any time. Calling Anderson on her cell, she waited, wondering what she would wear.

"Hello?"

Her heart gained speed at that deep voice in her ear.

"I'll go to Austin with you. Whatever it takes."

"Well, now, that's the best news I've heard all day. I'll be there in about an hour. How's that?"

"I'll be ready."

"Oh, and I wanted you to know the sheriff is keeping the deputy posted out there for the rest of the week. Just as a precaution."

"I'm glad to hear that. I didn't want to leave everyone here without some sort of human security."

"Consider it done. I'll see you soon, but remember…I can't really discuss my business at the capitol."

"Got it." She hung up, holding a hand to her throat. She and Anderson had been forced together on the compound, but this would be the first time they'd left the property together. That scared her into action. Hair, makeup, something pretty to wear. And shoes—real shoes, not work boots. Even if she had an ugly task to perform, Anderson had included lunch in the trip.

How would they both act, away from the scene of the crime? Would he be completely official and professional? Should she maintain some sort of decorum and distance? Honestly, the grisly way they'd met made her wonder if they'd ever have any sort of future together.

That and the tenacious devotion Anderson had to his job.

* * *

Anderson smiled over at Jennifer, taking in her pretty blue sweater and cute knee-length denim tiered skirt, worn with dark tights and tall brown boots. Tall brown boots with tall skinny heels. How did women walk in those things, anyway?

"You sure clean up nice."

"Thanks." She looked shy and unsure, but she was here in his truck, at least. Even if the woman was clutching her purse with white knuckles. Did he make her that nervous? Or was it this investigation and her fear of possibly seeing the face of the man who'd attacked her?

Reaching across to her, he said, "Hey, it's okay. Let's just relax. The end is in sight."

"I'm trying." She'd worn her hair down. It shimmered and bounced each time the truck jostled over the interstate toward Austin. "I'm glad things have settled down some. I mean, at least the destruction and digging can stop now. That you've found what they were looking for."

Her eyes went dark even as she spoke those words.

"Still missing Roscoe?" he asked, wishing he could take away her pain.

She bobbed her head. "I keep looking at his empty bed but I don't have the heart to put it out of sight yet. It's gonna be hard, after Mom leaves and…when you leave."

Anderson thought the same thing. "I might leave the compound, Jennifer, but I am not leaving you."

"I bet you say that to all the people you serve and protect."

"No, ma'am, I do not. Mainly because not all of them have pretty brown eyes and hair that looks like dark silk." He grimaced. "That sounded so corny, didn't it?"

She laughed, her smile crinkling her cheeks enough to show off two sweet dimples. "Lame, but nice to hear. And I don't smell like straw and animal, I hope."

"You smell like a bouquet," he said, sniffing the air near her. "But you're way too far over on that side of the truck."

She laughed again. "I'll stay over here for now, Ranger-man. I don't want to distract you."

He cut his eyes toward her. "Like I said, you've been doing that since the first day I saw you."

She leaned her head back on the seat. "That seems like a lifetime ago, doesn't it?"

He nodded, then took an exit ramp off I-35 and headed to the left. "Yep. A lot has happened since that day."

One thing being, he'd finally found someone who made him stop and think about something besides his work. But he was still trying to figure how that would play out.

"Any word on who was buried on my property?"

That brought him back to the here and now. "No. We'll go to headquarters first and get the mug shots out of the way. They might have heard something from the crime lab by now."

Anderson thought about Senator Huffington. Levi had agreed to meet him at the senator's office so they could question him together. "You can stroll around the grounds and check out the cafeteria and gift shop, but stay close, okay?"

"Just the grounds? I planned to walk around SoCo."

"Sorry, you need to stay on the capitol grounds. Too many variables on South Congress. When I'm out of my meeting, we'll walk to the restaurant I mentioned. It's not far from the capitol and it's in the SoCo district."

"All right. I can't wait to get a latte and take in some of the shops."

He pulled into a nondescript but modern-looking building. "We're here. Don't be nervous. Everyone's working on this investigation so any information is important."

She swallowed and opened her door. Anderson came around and helped her out of the truck.

A few minutes later, Jennifer was sitting in a ranger conference room going through book after book of mug shots. She'd met some of the other Rangers but the faces and names all merged inside her head.

"Any luck?" Anderson asked, stopping his paperwork to glance over at her. "You want something to drink?"

"No and no," she said, the tension mounting inside her head each time she turned the pages. "I don't think he's here, Anderson."

"We can bring in a forensic artist," he said. "Cade is going to do that with the skeleton we found. Her name is Paige Bryant. You'd like her."

"I'm not sure I'm up to that today, unless you think it's necessary."

He looked down at his watch. "I don't have time to set it up, anyway. I have to meet Levi at the capitol. But… keep that in mind for the future."

After going through several more books, she'd given up and let out a sigh. Part of her had hoped for a match.

"I'm sorry," Anderson said, glancing over at Jennifer.

"Why are you apologizing? I'm the one who couldn't identify that man."

"It's okay. You didn't get a very good look."

"No, I was too busy trying to stay alive. But I remember his eyes. I remember the hatred I saw there."

"C'mon," he said. "Let's get out of here."

He escorted her past all the curious faces and out the door without another word.

Anderson had wanted their time together to take her mind off losing Roscoe and everything else that had happened. And he'd prayed for another break in this case. Since nothing had panned out at headquarters, he'd have to focus on the business card he'd found inside the dirty jacket. He had a bad feeling that the honorable senator might not be so honorable after all. Could Huffington be involved with the Lions?

Levi McDonnell met Anderson in the Capitol Rotunda, shaking hands with him over the Six Flags of Texas seal embedded on the floor. France, Spain, Mexico, the United States, the Confederacy and the Republic of Texas flags all circled the round seal that depicted the Alamo and other aspects of Texas history.

"How ya doing?" Levi asked, his jet black hair glistening underneath the lights. "How's Jennifer?"

"We're both hanging in there," Anderson replied. "She couldn't find a match on her attacker. She's here but I told her to stay near the gift shop and cafeteria. I'm taking her for lunch after we talk to the senator."

"He knows we're coming," Levi said, leading the way to the elevators and the senator's office on the third floor. "But he has no idea why we're coming."

"Oh, I just bet he does," Anderson replied. "I'm guessing he won't talk even if he does know something."

"Good guess," Levi retorted as they stepped off the elevator.

After they'd announced themselves and shown their IDs to the senator's assistant, they were led to his swank office.

"Gentlemen," Senator Fred Huffington said, getting up to come around his desk and shake their hands. "It ain't every day I get a request to talk to two distinguished Texas Rangers. To what do I owe this pleasure?"

Anderson thought the man was laying it on a bit thick with the good ol' boy talk, but he played along. "Same here, Senator. We rarely come into the inner sanctuary of the President Pro Tem of the Texas Senate. Nice view."

The senator's smile faltered just a tad but he kept it pasted on his handsome face anyway. "It has its perks. Let's get on with it, then. I'm due for a vote this afternoon."

Levi and Anderson sat down and explained the situation about the intruder and the business card, bringing him up to speed on the drug trafficking they were investigating without mentioning the Lions. "And so, sir, do you have any idea how that man could have got your card?"

Anderson watched for signs of recognition, for some sort of clue. But the statesman was as cool as the wind blowing against the capitol's big pink limestone walls. Either he was a practiced liar or he didn't have any inkling of the cartel or the man who'd tried to get to the body.

The senator sat on the edge of his desk, his hands clasped. "Honestly, gentlemen, I have no idea. I hand out cards to constituents all the time." He shrugged as if to say "and that's that."

"Have you been to any gatherings recently where a mixed crowd might be? We have reason to believe this man is an illegal." Levi centered his brown eyes on the senator while he gave the description Anderson had included in his report. "Maybe you met him at an outdoors function, not a fancy dinner."

"I get what you're asking, son," the senator replied, his voice just below testy. "Like I said, boys, I travel all over our great state and I don't recall anyone in particular. The man you described could be anyone, anywhere in Texas. I don't think I can help you."

Anderson took note of the growing impatience in the man's tone. His gut told him the good senator knew more but had no intention of confessing right here on capitol grounds. They'd have to do some more research.

"Thanks for your time, sir," he said, getting up.

Levi gave Anderson a knowing look and shook the senator's hand. "We'll let you get to that vote."

"All right, then. Always good to see a Ranger. I don't

cotton to drug trafficking but we all know it's hard to break up a cartel coming over the border, no matter how many men we put on the patrol. You gentlemen let me know if I can help in any other way."

"I'll hold you to that, Senator," Anderson said, tipping his hat to the tall man who watched them out the door.

"I think he's lying," Levi said on a low voice when they exited the elevator.

"Careful," Anderson replied. "We're in the whispering gallery, remember?" The rotunda was called that because a whisper on one side could be heard clear on the other side.

Levi rolled his eyes. "I still think—"

"Me, too. But he ain't talking today, that's for sure. All the more reason to keep an eye on the man."

"Let me do some research," Levi replied. "That way, you can go have that lunch date with your lady."

"She's not exactly my lady," Anderson retorted. "Yet."

Jennifer glanced behind for the hundredth time. She'd enjoyed a cup of coffee, shopped for trinkets in the gift shop, and even bought her mother a pair of dangling Lone Star earrings.

And now, she was pretty sure she was being followed.

She'd first caught glances of a dark-haired man with a mustache behind her as she'd looked back after leaving the gift shop to get some fresh air. Afraid to attract attention inside the building, she'd found a side door and escaped outside, hoping she was just imagining things.

But she'd just spotted that same man coming across the grounds, headed straight toward her.

Now, her hands shaking as she stopped in front of the Heroes of the Alamo monument, she stood underneath a small live oak tree and worked her fingers on her phone to call Anderson.

"Anderson, it's me," she said when she heard his voice. "I'm outside. I think someone's following me."

"Where are you?"

She could tell he was running by the sound of his voice and the echo of noise following him.

"I'm near a tree right by the Heroes of the Alamo monument. What should I do?"

"Get behind either the tree or the monument. Stay where you are and whatever you do, don't take off running. He could take a shot. Stay on the line, Jennifer, do you hear me?"

"I will." She took a deep breath, hurried around the monument, then looked back. "He's a few feet away. Dark hair with a mustache. I think it's the man who attacked me." She let out a gasp. "And he has a gun."

EIGHTEEN

Anderson's pulse slapped at his temple with each pounding of his boots against granite as he raced down the steps and headed out onto the grounds. His gun drawn but down, he shouted "Texas Ranger. Get out of the way."

People moved over, shocked and dazed, as he rushed through the tourists strolling down the long alleyway of monuments and trees known as the Great Walk in front of the capitol entrance. Squinting into the afternoon sun, Anderson frantically searched until he saw the Alamo monument. But where was Jennifer?

And where was the man after her?

Anderson slowed, stopped and focused on the area around the monument. He spotted a lone man wearing a wool sock cap slowly making his way toward the monument.

Was Jennifer behind the granite base?

Anderson watched the man, noting the deliberate cadence of the man's steps. The man was medium height and he had a dark mustache. Jennifer thought this was her attacker and Anderson believed her.

Berating himself for putting Jennifer in danger,

Anderson stayed a few steps behind the man, oblivious now to the crowd of people forming in a cluster up near the steps. He looked from the man to the monument. Jennifer couldn't be inside the open passageway underneath the arched columns. That would put her in danger. Maybe she'd gone behind a tree or one of the wide columns supporting the bronze statue of the Alamo soldier holding up a musket.

Breathing hard, Anderson centered his gaze on the man. He couldn't shoot him in the back, but he could bring him to a halt before he got to Jennifer.

Then the man made a quick move and disappeared behind the monument. Anderson took off, drawing his gun out from his body. When he heard a scream, Anderson knew the suspect had found Jennifer.

Jennifer gagged at the moist grimy hand wrapped over her mouth, her nostrils flaring with fear, the smell of dirty clothes and foul breath making her feel queasy.

The man said something in Spanish then leaned close. "Don't make a sound."

Jennifer recognized that voice but she did as he said, praying Anderson would find her at the same time she hoped he'd stay out of the line of this man's gun sight. She bobbed her head, closing her eyes to the terror surrounding her.

She could see the blue sky, hear laughter somewhere out on the grounds, could smell the scents of fresh-cut grass and decaying leaves mixed with the stench of sweat and grime, and all the while her heart bumped and pushed for escape. This man wanted her dead because she'd seen his face. Was he that desperate or that dangerous? Maybe both.

But she hadn't come this far to die right here on such a beautiful fall day. She had God on her side now. And she had Anderson. So she shifted her perspective from that of a victim to that of a survivor. Glancing around as the man dragged her up against one of the marble columns, Jennifer felt the warmth of the sun on her face.

And the touch of God's love.

"We have to get out of here," the man said, his English broken and heavily accented. "*Si, querida?* You've seen me too many times now. Too many times."

So this was the man who'd been at the alligator pond the day she'd found the cut fence and the man who attacked her. She couldn't go with him. She knew if she did so, she'd die. She'd never see her mother or Anderson again.

The man glanced around the big column then yanked her close, pushing her toward a copse of trees off the path.

Jennifer grunted, almost stumbling as he forced her into a twisted run, his gun burning into her sweater near her ribcage. Looking around for a weapon, she turned back toward the monument, praying someone would notice she was being taken by force.

That's when she saw a familiar face.

Anderson.

But his face had changed. He looked dangerous and determined and angry. She saw it all there in the briefest of glimpses, but it was enough for now.

Jennifer didn't dare let on that she'd seen him, but her heart shifted and picked up a new beat with each step into the trees.

And then she heard Anderson call out. "Texas Ranger. Drop the weapon and let the woman go."

After that, her world tilted and shifted as the man holding her whirled around and shot at Anderson, using her as a shield while he did it. But Anderson was ready for the shot. He ducked into some shrubs, his big body rolling as he landed.

The man urged Jennifer on, cursing in Spanish, fear and frustration causing him to perspire.

Jennifer didn't dare try to get away now. He'd kill her and Anderson, too.

They hurried across the vast acreage. Where was Anderson? Had he been hit?

They'd reached a grouping of live oaks, the air going dark in the shelter of the great trees. Jennifer had to do something to save herself before this man took her off the grounds and into the downtown crowd.

So she stopped abruptly, shifting her frame against the surprised man, forcing him to grab her. And when he did, Jennifer managed to hold her hands together and elbow him with a thrust to his stomach. It wasn't much, but it caused him to struggle and loosen his grip on the gun.

Anderson watched from his spot around the corner. He'd managed to sneak through the trees and wait, hoping to meet the attacker and Jennifer head-on. Now, he held his breath as he stood hidden behind a massive live oak trunk, and watched Jennifer struggling against her captor.

And that diversion gave Anderson just enough time to step out, take aim, and wait for the perfect moment.

It came as the man turned away from Jennifer, holding her with one hand as he blasted her in guttural Spanish.

"Let her go!" Anderson listened, held up his gun and put his sights on the man. He'd only have one shot. Better make it a good one. When the man grabbed Jennifer again, Anderson didn't hesitate.

The shot rang out, echoing through the trees.

And the man holding Jennifer went down into a heap on the leaf-covered grass.

Jennifer gulped in fresh air, the sound of the single shot ringing inside her head. She put her hands to her mouth then stared down at the open eyes of the man who'd just tried to kidnap her. Blood ran from his midsection, just below his heart. She gasped, fell down on the leaves and grass a few feet from the man, then closed her eyes.

But two big arms brought her up. "It's all right. It's over now. He won't hurt you. No one will ever hurt you again."

She sank against Anderson's suede jacket, the feel of his badge crushing against her heart, the warmth of his arms protecting her giving her a new hope, a new beginning and a reason to believe.

Two hours later, after they'd given statements to the capitol security, the Austin police and everyone else involved, Anderson thanked Levi for coming back to the scene and took Jennifer by the arm to walk her back to his truck.

He'd have more reports to file and more questions to answer, but for now, Jennifer was safe. And he wanted nothing more than to get her out of here and home.

"Do we know who that man was?" she asked once they were in the truck and on the road.

Anderson nodded. "We ran an electronic fingerprint scan. Name's Alfred Lando. Got a record for small-time drug trafficking and other petty crimes. He's not an illegal but he has ties back in Mexico."

"He's the one, Anderson," she said, her hands in her lap. "I can at least identify him now." She looked beat and tired, her clothes rumpled and dirty. And they never did have their lunch.

"Yes. It's over now. Hey, you hungry?"

"No." She searched his face. "Do you think that man was involved in vandalizing the rescue center?"

"I can't say for sure, but that's a good assumption."

She let that soak in, her face going pale. "Is this really the end? Or will they keep coming after me?"

"I think this is it," he replied. "Too much heat on them right now." When his phone beeped, he pulled it out. "Let me get this, okay?"

She pulled her hands closer around her and fell silent.

"Michaels."

Anderson listened while Senator Fred Huffington read him the riot act in a very colorful dressing down.

"What in the name of Texas were you thinking, Ranger, engaging in a shoot-out on capitol grounds?"

Anderson let out a frustrated sigh. "I was doing my job, sir. The suspect had a woman at gunpoint. I had to step in."

"Listen, I read the report and got an update from my aide, but I don't like this one bit. Now whatever y'all are investigating, you'd better keep it away from my door, understand? The good people of Texas expect us to protect them, not shoot people right in front of tourists and citizens in our halls of government. You got me, son?"

Anderson got it loud and clear. He'd touched a nerve with the President Pro Tem. Now why did that not surprise him? "I did what I had to do, sir. And I was protecting one of your tax-paying citizens today."

"Yeah, and I'm sure you'll be hailed a hero. But you could have handled this differently. Should have brought in backup and let our security officers help you."

Anderson gritted his teeth. "I immediately alerted your security staff. They kept the crowd back and called in backup. Sorry, I have to go, sir. I appreciate the suggestions." He disconnected and glanced over at Jennifer. She was his priority right now, not some possibly corrupt lawmaker who was afraid of the heat.

Jennifer shifted on the seat. "Am I still in danger?"

Anderson couldn't give her a definite on that even though he was pretty sure she was safe now. He'd told her the danger was over and almost lost her because of that. "I want to say yes, but I don't want anymore surprises like the one we had today."

"I see," she said, her tone full of defeat.

"Look, once we put out the word that Lando was killed in downtown Austin, on capitol grounds, I think the heat will be too high for anyone to come after you. We have the unidentified body and we've killed one of their own trying to harm you because you could identify him. Your property is too hot for them to ever come near it again."

She didn't look convinced.

Anderson's heart fell like a lead weight to his stomach. Could he lose Jennifer because of this never-ending case?

From the look on her face right now, yes, he certainly could.

NINETEEN

Two days later, Anderson looked impatiently at his watch, then at the men filing around the conference room located in a big law office in San Antonio.

"Relax, buddy," Daniel Riley said under his breath, giving Anderson a warning look, his dark eyes widening.

"I'd like to get this over with," Anderson said as the Alamo Planning Committee gathered to discuss the threatening letter Anderson had in his hand. "I need to get back to the case at hand."

"No, you want to get back to the subject at hand—one Jennifer Rodgers—from what Levi tells me."

"Levi needs to mind his own business," Anderson said, but it was without malice. His friends meant well, but he couldn't help but worry and fret about things best left unsaid.

Jennifer wasn't exactly taking his calls these days.

In fact, the woman had pretty much told him to come back and see her when he'd cracked this case. And not a minute sooner.

She wasn't afraid of the bad guys. She was afraid of loving him. Maybe because he'd brought danger to her door and the one time he'd taken her out of her comfortable environment, he'd almost gotten her killed. Or maybe the fact that he'd bragged over and over about his dedication to being a Ranger. No time for anything else. Maybe she decided she couldn't deal with that.

So much for a fun first date.

And that failure on his part rankled Anderson enough to make him jittery and restless. But he *did* have a job to do, as always. Right now, that job involved smoothing the feathers of these determined men by assuring them the Rangers would be there to serve and protect so they could have an all-out celebration for the 175th anniversary of the Battle of the Alamo.

While Anderson could only sit here and stew about the battle inside his heart.

He watched as oil baron Rodney Tanner and cattleman Hank Zarvy walked in wearing expensive suits, top-of-the-line hats and handmade boots. Tanner nodded, then settled into a chair across the way, his hawk-like gaze sweeping the room. Hank Zarvy went around shaking hands and grinning. Neither of them looked too worried about the letter Zarvy had handed over to the Rangers.

A letter that stated, "Call off the celebration or pay the consequences. A lot of people could get hurt."

Probably some extremist group wanting to protest or cause a ruckus. Whatever it was, Anderson wanted to get on with the reassuring and preparing so he could get back to figuring out Jennifer.

Then Sam Myers walked in the room, his dark gaze moving over the faces to settle on Anderson. When the man headed straight toward Anderson, he got up and held out his hand. "Mr. Myers, I'm Anderson Michaels. We spoke on the phone."

Sam Myers was gray-headed and tall, with a white mustache that matched his silver-shot hair. "Good to meet the man who saved my granddaughter," he said, extending Anderson a hearty handshake. "I recognize you from the pictures on the news and in the paper."

Several of the board members looked up at that declaration. Rodney Tanner leaned forward. "Sam, I didn't realize you had a granddaughter until I read in the paper about the attempt on her life at the capitol. Some vagrant wanting money—imagine that."

Mr. Myers nodded. "I'm not proud of it, but I haven't kept in touch with my daughter and her only child, Jennifer. Long story and a matter of wounded pride on my part. But thanks to this young man here alerting me to what happened, I think things are about to change on that front. Ranger Michaels is a true Texas hero."

Anderson saw Daniel's surprised grin and shot him a warning glare. While the kidnapping had been reported as a random mugging, he'd felt the need to give full disclosure when he called Sam Myers about this threat and this meeting. And besides, he wanted to bring Jennifer and her grandparents together for a lot of reasons, some selfish, some not so selfish.

He leaned close to Sam Myers. "Could we talk privately after the meeting, sir? About Jennifer?"

Sam nodded. "We have a lot to discuss, son."

Anderson returned to his seat, but he didn't miss the questioning glance Hank Zarvy sent him. Anderson didn't consider himself a hero.

And apparently, neither did Jennifer Rodgers.

* * *

She missed her hero.

Jennifer wondered for the hundredth time why she'd pushed Anderson away when she was so in love with the man it hurt to breathe.

Maybe because she couldn't handle being in love with a man who courted danger. Just like her father but in a different way. Or at least that's what Suzanne kept telling her.

"Honey, the man saved your life. And from the way he looks at you and tries to take care of you, I'd say he's got it bad for you, too."

Jennifer wasn't so sure she wanted to be taken care of if it meant having to watch Anderson go off and face that kind of intense danger every day. How could she live like that? Hadn't it been enough that her father had done the same thing, that each time he kissed her goodbye she couldn't be sure he'd come back?

And he hadn't come back from the Amazon.

What if she gave her heart to Anderson, kissed him goodbye and never saw him alive again? Being held at gunpoint the other day and watching Anderson shoot her captor right in front of her had only intensified her fears. Right along with her love for Anderson.

But the man had made it very clear he'd rather stick to the job than get involved. Too messy. Women didn't understand the nature of his work or the long hours.

Jennifer had certainly fallen into that category right from the get-go.

"I need some time," she'd told Anderson.

"I need some time," she repeated to her mother now as they finished up with the late feeding of the horses.

Jennifer looked around at the new lumber lined up behind the barn and the beginning of a new wall Anderson's father and his church buddies had already erected.

Everywhere she looked, she saw memories of Anderson.

How could she go on without him?

How could she live with him?

Anderson couldn't live like this.

After leaving San Antonio with a promise to continue looking into the threatening letter and keep watch over the committee's proceedings, he drove up the interstate toward Rodgers Exotic Animal Rescue, determined to talk to Jennifer. But he didn't do that. Yet. First, he had to let his mother and his family in on what was going on and enlist his mother's help.

He'd already had a long talk with Jennifer's formidable grandfather, but at least they'd reached an understanding.

And come up with this plan.

Now if he could just get Jennifer to cooperate.

He'd talk to Suzanne, too, since she seemed to be halfway in his corner. She also had to tread carefully in regards to her daughter, too. He'd just have to pray that he could make this work.

Jennifer got up at the usual time on Saturday morning, her list of chores front and center on her mind as she entered the kitchen.

Suzanne was waiting along with Jacob and Becky and two of Jennifer's most reliable volunteers.

"What's up?" she asked, afraid another animal had died. Or worse, another set of human bones had been found.

Suzanne smiled and handed her a cup of steaming coffee. "You have a card here, honey. Now read it and follow the instructions. We're taking over again today so you can have a Saturday off."

"I don't want a Saturday off," Jennifer said on a stubborn groan. "I need to work, Mom."

"You think you need to work," Becky chimed in, looking spunky and determined. "But what you need is to read this card and do exactly as it says. We have our orders."

"And who gave you these orders?"

"Can't say," Suzanne retorted. "Just do it, Jenny. We'll take care of things, we promise."

With that, she motioned to the others and they were out the door before Jennifer could protest. Frustrated and still half asleep, Jennifer sank down at the table and watched the gold and cream sunrise coming over the hills just outside the back door. Then she tore open the envelope and pulled out the pretty floral card.

"We never had our lunch date. Get dressed in something pretty and bring a coat. I'm taking you on a picnic. I'll be there at eight sharp. Don't make me have to drag you out of that compound, Jennifer."

The man had such as sweet way of asking—no, telling—her what to do.

Jennifer's first inclination was to throw the card in the trash and go muck stables.

But…she didn't really want to muck stables or feed Boudreaux and Bobby Wayne, or check on the turtles.

And it was all Anderson Michaels' fault.

"Okay, Ranger-man," she said, staring at the scrawled black ink on the card. "Just one date. Just to remember you with a good ending. And then that's it."

"Where are we going?" she asked Anderson an hour later. She was once again in his big truck, snuggled in a long brown sweater-coat and her favorite jeans and yet another pair of boots—these sturdy and flat and good for long walks.

"I thought it was about time you see where I grew up," he said, his grin telling her that he seemed glad she'd agreed to this.

"You're taking me to…the ranch? Your family's ranch?"

"Yep."

"Will we be alone there?"

"I sure hope so. At least, we will after I give all of 'em a chance to fuss over you a little bit."

"I don't need fussing over, Ranger-man."

"Oh, yes, ma'am, you most certainly do."

"I'm not the fuss-over type."

"Get used to it," he said, taking her hand.

Then he pulled up to a sprawling yellow-brick ranch house with two live oaks centered on each side of the wide front porch. "This is it—the Michaels residence. I have a little cabin on the creek. I'll show you that later."

Jennifer braced herself for what was about to come. She was finally getting a chance to see how a real family lived. But she wasn't sure she could handle that right now without blurting out to Anderson that she never wanted to leave this place. Or him.

An hour later, Jennifer had enjoyed homemade cinnamon rolls and laughter and small talk and a tour of the big house and a walk through Ramona's fall garden.

Now, she was holding Anderson's hand and strolling toward the tiny cabin set back near a lone cottonwood tree beside a gurgling creek bed. The woods around them were ablaze in an autumn fire of burgundy, orange and gold.

Anderson set down the big basket of food his mother had packed and turned toward Jennifer.

"Finally, I have you alone."

He pulled her close, wrapping his arms around her, holding her. The air was chilly, but the sun and his nearness warmed Jennifer. She wanted to stay in his arms for a long, long time.

He lifted away, staring down at her with those bright golden eyes. "I'm not good with words, but...I need to tell you a few things."

"I'm listening," she said, her heart unfurling like a falling leaf.

"First, I love you. I think I've loved you since I watched you feeding those two ornery alligators."

She couldn't speak, couldn't take her eyes off his face.

"And second, because I love you, I want the best for you. And that means...I've done something that's probably going to make you mad. Real mad."

"What?" she asked, her hope floating away with the creek's gentle current.

"This," he said, turning her around as an older couple

came walking toward them. "I invited your grandparents to share this picnic with us."

Anderson watched from his perch against the cotton-wood tree while Jennifer sat at the picnic table talking quietly with Sam and Martha Myers. Had he done the right thing?

He hoped so. Suzanne had approved this daring attempt to reunite Jennifer with the Myers and she'd had her own long talk with her parents earlier today.

Praying this would work, Anderson enjoyed watching her face each time Sam Myers asked her yet another question about the rescue farm. Was she happy? Or was she just being polite to save face? Would she ream him out once her grandparents were gone?

When Sam Myers stood up, Anderson came off the tree and held his breath. Then he watched in amazement as the old man opened his arms to his granddaughter.

Jennifer stood, too, and hesitated for just a second.

Then she rushed into her grandfather's embrace, tears streaming down her face. Soon, Mrs. Myers was hugging her close, too.

Anderson stayed in his spot until they'd said their goodbyes. But Sam Myers turned and tipped his hat to Anderson before he took his wife's arm and escorted her back toward the ranch house.

"Can you believe it?" Jennifer said later, half of her veggie sandwich still on the paper plate in front of her. "They want to set up a foundation, Anderson, for me. For the rescue farm. A huge, huge foundation with lots and lots of real money in it. Was I wrong to accept that?"

"No, you were right, darlin'. They want to make amends and, granted, it took seeing your face on the news and hearing what happened to you to bring them around, but Jennifer, this means you'll be safe there again. You can get a proper security system, put up new pens, hire full-time helpers, and rebuild whatever you want. I'd say this is a win-win situation."

"I just can't get over the generosity—first your parents and your church. Now my grandparents. And they want to come by tomorrow and have a tour. Grandma's bringing lunch for Mom and me." She smiled, her eyes watering again.

"I was afraid you'd be mad," he admitted, glad to see her pretty smile.

"I was at first, but…how can I stay mad at a man who's gone out of his way to save me? And when I say save me, I don't mean just from the drug cartel or the grumpy neighbor. You saved me from myself. You showed me the way back to my faith and my family. How can I be mad about that?"

He came around the table and tugged her up and into his arms. "And let's not forget the best part. I love you. It would be nice if you felt the same."

She leaned up and kissed him. "I didn't want to love you. I fought against it."

"I know. You think I'm a thrill seeker like your daddy, right?"

"Aren't you? Didn't you tell me over and over you can't have a real relationship with a woman?"

"Jennifer, going after criminals doesn't give me a

thrill. I hate every minute of the ugliness I have to deal with. But it's worth it to me to do my job. I took an oath to do that and to protect the people of Texas. It's fulfilling and satisfying and yes, it's dangerous, so I can't bluff my way out of that. But, honey, you frighten me a whole lot more than chasing criminals. And in spite of my big talk on staying single, if you don't agree to love me back, I'll be a broken man. Do you want that on your conscience?"

She smiled up at him. "Well, since you put it that way…I guess not." Then she put her hands on his face and brought his head down. "I love you, too, Rangerman. I'm pretty sure I'd be a lot more miserable without you than with you. And here's the evidence."

She proceeded to kiss him, showing him in no uncertain terms that she meant it.

Anderson's heart fussed and fumed and explored with a love so strong that he thought he might dance right out of his boots.

"It's gonna be all right now," he told her. "You'll be safe. We'll be working with Paige Bryant to identify the body we found. Cade will investigate that. We won't quit until we find out who murdered Gregory Pike. But you and I will have a lot more time together. I can't promise bad things won't happen, but you'll have me around for a long, long time."

"I'll hold you to that," she said, kissing him again.

Then Anderson heard a yelp and lifted his mouth from hers. "What was that?"

Jennifer stepped away and turned her head. "Sounded like an animal."

"Sure did." He tried to hide his smile.

The yelping started back up. "It's coming from over there." He pointed toward the stables. "Let's go see."

Together, they hurried across the pasture.

And then a tiny chocolate-colored puppy came loping out of the tall grass next to the barn, his curious nose wet as he flopped and fell over his big feet.

Jennifer looked at the puppy, then back to Anderson. "Oh, how adorable. Where'd he come from?"

"I have no idea," Anderson said, trying to stay cool. "We get a lot of strays out here. People come by and drop them off. Looks like we got ourselves another mouth to feed."

He watched, love coloring his world in vivid shades of gold and amber, as Jennifer fell on the grass and lifted the curious little dog up into her lap. "I think he's a chocolate lab. Isn't he beautiful?"

"Beautiful," Anderson said, walking toward them, his eyes on her.

Jennifer held the puppy close, letting him nuzzle her face. "Are you gonna keep him, Anderson? Please don't send him to the pound."

"Wouldn't dream of it," Anderson said, reaching down to rub the dog's head. "He needs a good home, don't you think?"

Jennifer looked up at him then, her expression changing as realization washed over her. "I've been set up, haven't I?"

"I don't know what you mean."

She reached out a hand and yanked him down beside her. The puppy took that as a sign to play so he frolicked around in a circle, his chubby legs dancing between Anderson and Jennifer while he yelped in delight.

"Oh, I think you know exactly what I mean. That's twice—no, the third time—today you've sprung something on me. You're very demanding and sneaky, you know."

"How am I doing so far?"

She leaned close, the little lab trying to push between them. "I think I'm beginning to love surprises and demands and a tad of sneakiness."

Anderson pulled a hand through her hair. "Then I'd say our life together will be real interesting, darlin'."

"I can't wait," she said. Then she dropped her smile. "I miss Roscoe, Anderson. But the puppy is so cute."

"Maybe you can get to know him and if you like him, the little rascal can be yours. When you're ready."

"Rascal. That's a good name."

"For the dog, you mean?"

"For the dog and for a certain Ranger, too, I think."

Anderson kissed her again. "Good enough." Better than good. This was near perfect. Rascal yelped in agreement and went back to playing with his new family.

* * * * *

Love Inspired®
SUSPENSE

TITLES AVAILABLE NEXT MONTH

Available March 8, 2011

MISSION: OUT OF CONTROL
Missions of Mercy
Susan May Warren

FACE OF DANGER
Texas Ranger Justice
Valerie Hansen

CODE OF JUSTICE
Liz Johnson

DOUBLE IDENTITY
Diane Burke

LISCNM0211

REQUEST YOUR FREE BOOKS!

2 FREE RIVETING INSPIRATIONAL NOVELS PLUS 2 FREE MYSTERY GIFTS

Love Inspired®
SUSPENSE

Read on for a sneak peek of FACE OF DANGER
by Valerie Hansen, the next exciting book in the
Texas Ranger Justice series available March,
only from Love Inspired Suspense.

The usually busy Texas Ranger headquarters building in Austin was quiet—except for the beating of forensic artist Paige Bryant's heart and her niggling feeling that something wasn't quite right.

"Stop it. You're being silly," she told herself as she leaned out of her studio and peered down the empty hallway. It looked as though everyone in that part of the office had already gone home for the night. Which was where she should be. Where she *would* be if she weren't waiting for a delivery.

She closed her office door and began to pace. It was only about seventy-five miles from Company D in San Antonio to this main Ranger office in Austin, and easy, highway driving almost all the way. What could be keeping that Ranger? She didn't know Sergeant Cade Jarvis well, but the few times they had met she'd been favorably impressed.

Paige huffed, disgusted with herself. *Impressed?* Boy, was that an understatement. If Sergeant Jarvis was half as good-looking as she recalled, he'd be attractive enough to curl her toes. He stood nearly six feet tall, with dusky blond hair and mischievous eyes the color of warm mocha java.

She was about to give up on him when her phone rang. "Hello?"

"Ms. Bryant? This is Cade Jarvis," the vibrant male voice said. "I'm going to be a little late."

He was already more than a little late, but something in his tone gave Paige pause and made her ask, "Are you all right?"

"I was run off the road not far from there."

"Oh, no! Are you all right?"

"Fine. Actually, I'm in better shape than my truck is. I'll hitch a ride with one of the troopers and have him drop me at your office."

"Are you sure you're okay?"

"Yeah. Thankfully, there's no problem with the remains I'm bringing you, either. I had the skull packed in a padded evidence bag, so it wasn't damaged by the collision. I figured you'd probably make a composite copy to model the clay over, anyway, but I'd still like to get it to you in one piece. I should be at your office within a half hour. Do you mind waiting just a little longer?"

"Not at all, Sergeant. See you soon."

To see if Cade and Paige can figure out the identity of the remains found on Jennifer Rodger's property, pick up FACE OF DANGER by Valerie Hansen available March, only from Love Inspired Suspense.